the perfect secret

(a jessie hunt psychological suspense—book 11)

blake pierce

Blake Pierce

Blake Pierce is the USA Today bestselling author of the RILEY PAGE mystery series, which includes seventeen books. Blake Pierce is also the author of the MACKENZIE WHITE mystery series, comprising fourteen books; of the AVERY BLACK mystery series, comprising six books; of the KERI LOCKE mystery series, comprising five books; of the MAKING OF RILEY PAIGE mystery series, comprising six books; of the KATE WISE mystery series, comprising seven books; of the CHLOE FINE psychological suspense mystery, comprising six books; of the JESSE HUNT psychological suspense thriller series, comprising fourteen books (and counting); of the AU PAIR psychological suspense thriller series, comprising three books; of the ZOE PRIME mystery series, comprising four books (and counting); of the new ADELE SHARP mystery series, comprising six books (and counting); of the EUROPEAN VOYAGE cozy mystery series, comprising six books (and counting); of the LAURA FROST FBI suspense thriller, comprising three books (and counting); and of the ELLA DARK FBI suspense thriller, comprising three books (and counting).

An avid reader and lifelong fan of the mystery and thriller genres, Blake loves to hear from you, so please feel free to visit www.blakepierceauthor.com to learn more and stay in touch.

TAKING (Book #4)
STALKING (Book #5)
KILLING (Book #6)

RILEY PAIGE MYSTERY SERIES
ONCE GONE (Book #1)
ONCE TAKEN (Book #2)
ONCE CRAVED (Book #3)
ONCE LURED (Book #4)
ONCE HUNTED (Book #5)
ONCE PINED (Book #6)
ONCE FORSAKEN (Book #7)
ONCE COLD (Book #8)
ONCE STALKED (Book #9)
ONCE LOST (Book #10)
ONCE BURIED (Book #11)
ONCE BOUND (Book #12)
ONCE TRAPPED (Book #13)
ONCE DORMANT (Book #14)
ONCE SHUNNED (Book #15)
ONCE MISSED (Book #16)
ONCE CHOSEN (Book #17)

MACKENZIE WHITE MYSTERY SERIES
BEFORE HE KILLS (Book #1)
BEFORE HE SEES (Book #2)
BEFORE HE COVETS (Book #3)
BEFORE HE TAKES (Book #4)
BEFORE HE NEEDS (Book #5)
BEFORE HE FEELS (Book #6)
BEFORE HE SINS (Book #7)
BEFORE HE HUNTS (Book #8)
BEFORE HE PREYS (Book #9)
BEFORE HE LONGS (Book #10)
BEFORE HE LAPSES (Book #11)
BEFORE HE ENVIES (Book #12)
BEFORE HE STALKS (Book #13)
BEFORE HE HARMS (Book #14)

AVERY BLACK MYSTERY SERIES
CAUSE TO KILL (Book #1)

PROLOGUE

He wasn't supposed to be there.

Under normal circumstances Cord Mahoney would never have come near this part of the mansion. But the guest house where he was crashing was clear across the estate and he knew he'd never make it in time.

He'd tried every guest bathroom he could find in the house, but at a party with more than five hundred revelers, they all had long lines. So he'd snuck up to Jasper's private wing, the one area that was off limits to guests, which meant it was also the one area with an available toilet.

Even in his drunken, uninhibited state, part of him worried that Jasper would kick him out of the guest house he was letting him stay in if he found him up here. It wasn't a ridiculous concern. Jasper Otis was a notoriously volatile guy, and as a billionaire dozens of times over, he could afford to be.

But when you have to go, you have to go. That's how Cord found himself stumbling past the mahogany doors into Jasper's private wing and clumsily tiptoeing through the man's massive bedroom toward the closed door that he desperately prayed hid a bathroom. If it didn't, he was going to be reduced to using a trash can.

He pushed open the door, turned on the light, and almost cheered out loud when he saw the toilet. He hurried over and relieved himself just in time, though his aim wasn't perfect because of his unintentional swaying. Then he moved to the sink to wash his hands. As he dried them off, he glanced in the mirror and saw the large shower behind him. It was about the size of a sauna and even had a marble bench built into the back wall.

Then he noticed something else. At first, he doubted what he was seeing, maybe because the room was spinning slightly. But when he squinted, it was still there. Lying on the shower floor near the bench was a woman, wearing just a bra and a long, black skirt with a slit up the side. She looked like she'd passed out. That wouldn't have stunned Cord. Jasper's parties were infamous for all kinds of wildness: live bands, endless booze, copious amounts of drugs, bikini-clad young women, and occasional orgies. So seeing a half-naked woman crashed

1

out in a shower stall wasn't as shocking as some might think. Seeing her like that in Jasper's shower was.

Cord called out to her quietly to see if he could rouse her, but she didn't respond. She was lying on her back, which could be a choking hazard if she threw up, so he peeked through the glass to make sure she hadn't. He saw nothing other than a reasonably attractive woman in her early forties. She was no bikini girl, but at Jasper's parties, it took all kinds.

He did notice that her head was bent at an awkward angle that would leave a nasty ache in her neck when she woke up. He decided that the gentlemanly thing to do was to shake her slightly so she could readjust her position. So he opened the glass door, bent down, and gave her a gentle jostle on her shoulder. Her skin was wet. He looked down and saw that her clothes were too, along with the shower floor. He gave her another little shove. She didn't react—at all.

That's when Cord noticed that she wasn't breathing. Panic welled up inside him but he managed to force it down long enough to remember the CPR training from his junior lifeguard days. He got out his phone, dialed 911, put it on speaker, and rested it on the shower bench. Then he moved beside her and prepared to start compressions.

He was about to press down on her chest for the first time when he noticed something else. Her neck wasn't just bent awkwardly. It was lolling to the side sloppily, as if there was nothing supporting it. If he didn't know better he'd think it was broken.

It was just as the 911 operator came on the line that he realized it was. That's when he began to scream.

2

CHAPTER ONE

Jessie Hunt officially gave up on sleep at 5:10 a.m.

She'd been awake since four anyway and there didn't seem to be any point in lying in bed, especially today. So she got up and quietly made her way out to the kitchen to start the coffee.

Jessie's half-sister, Hannah, wasn't an early riser under any circumstances, but certainly not on a Sunday morning. And since she'd just started her senior year of high school, weekends were especially precious to her. Jessie did her best to be respectful of that, if for no other reason than to keep the peace.

It was easier to avoid accidentally waking anyone up since the big move. It had been a month since they'd left the apartment of Jessie's best friend, Kat, and started to settle in at the house Jessie had inherited from her mentor and friend, Garland Moses. There was lots more space and the walls were thicker.

The new house had an added benefit. As a one-story home formerly occupied by a long-widowed senior citizen, it was already well-designed for people with mobility challenges. That was a major plus considering that Jessie's boyfriend, LAPD Detective Ryan Hernandez, was coming home today.

Nearly six weeks after being stabbed in the chest by Jessie's ex-husband and four weeks after being taken out of a medically induced coma and removed from a ventilator, he'd been given approval to leave the hospital. Jessie's excitement when Dr. Badalia gave her the news was tempered by his warning that the hardest part of Ryan's recovery had yet to begin.

He would need multiple daily visits from a nurse to help out and evaluate his progress, in addition to daily physical therapy. Dr. Badalia had suggested a full-time, in-home nurse for a few months but Ryan had balked at the idea. Jessie didn't want to make him feel powerless so she'd consented to his wishes. But she worried that even with all the equipment she'd had installed, including handrails, bath and toilet accessories, and help buttons in every room, she might still not be prepared for the responsibility.

3

Caring for a wheelchair-bound thirty-two-year-old man who might have cognitive impairment was a challenge on its own. Doing that while simultaneously raising a seventeen-year-old who was still recovering from seeing her adoptive parents murdered felt borderline insurmountable.

But it wasn't all darkness. Kat had been an amazing friend, offering her place as a safe haven after Jessie and Hannah couldn't return to the condo where Ryan had been stabbed. She'd also been a shoulder to lean on and someone to vent to, even as she was trying to keep her own fledgling private investigator business running.

Another good distraction for Jessie was work. After officially leaving her job as a criminal profiler for the LAPD, she had been teaching a weekly forensics seminar at USC, her alma mater. She was supposed to instruct a full-on class in the subject when the fall semester began a week from Monday.

In addition, she'd come to an informal agreement with her former boss, Central Station Police Captain Roy Decker. If time permitted, she'd offer her services as a profiling consultant on major cases. She'd already worked on two as part of the arrangement, one involving the death of a faded movie star and just last week, the murder of an abducted oil heiress.

But with Ryan's arrival later today and classes picking up in a week, she doubted she'd be able to help out much on the law enforcement front going forward. And if Hannah's reaction when Jessie told her she'd be expected to help out with Ryan—cursing under her breath—was any indication, just keeping her head above water was going to be job enough.

Her cell phone rang and she quickly silenced it. Even before looking at it, she knew that at this hour, the call could only be from one of two places. She was relieved to see it wasn't the hospital.

"Hey, Captain," she said. "A little early to be calling on a Sunday morning, don't you think? The sun's not even up."

"Sorry, Hunt," he replied, maintaining the last name formality even though she was no longer an employee. "You know I wouldn't reach out like this unless it was a big deal."

"Whatever it is, I'm think I'm going to have to take a pass on this one. I start teaching in a week. More importantly, Ryan leaves the hospital this afternoon."

"I know," he said. "That's why I need to see you this morning. Please—don't say no until you've heard what this is about."

4

Jessie wanted to say no. With everything going on at home, she didn't need the extra responsibility. And yet, she couldn't help but be curious. She relented slightly.

"See me? Can't you just fill me in over the phone?"

"No. This one's pretty sensitive. Can you be in my office in an hour, just to hear me out? Trust me—it'll be worth your while."

Jessie knew he was playing her. Captain Decker understood just which buttons to push to pique her interest. And it was working.

"This better be good," she warned, though she knew he wasn't intimidated.

He had her hooked.

*

As Jessie entered the station, she noticed that it was deathly quiet.

That wasn't a shock at 6:04 on a Sunday morning, but it was still unsettling to walk past the deputy desk sergeant, who was reading a magazine because there was no one in the lobby. It was odd not to hear the standard sounds of phone chatter and keyboard typing that usually filled the bullpen. Jessie passed the half dozen people sitting forlornly at their desks and headed for Decker's office.

Just before entering she checked her phone one more time. She didn't really expect a text from Hannah at this hour but she knew that when she got one, it wouldn't be friendly. Hannah was surly these days as it was. But when she saw the note on the kitchen counter saying that Jessie had gone to the station to discuss a case and to keep the house tidy for Ryan's arrival, her response was unlikely to be gracious enthusiasm.

Jessie knocked on the closed door to Decker's office.

"One minute," came the gruff response from the other side.

While she waited, Jessie glanced back at the HSS section of the bullpen to where she used to sit. Homicide Special Section was a unit within LAPD dedicated to cases that had high profiles or intense media scrutiny, often involving multiple victims and serial killers. For two years, she'd been the unit's primary profiler, working with a small team of detectives led by Ryan. They'd sat at desks across from each other, initially as partners, and eventually, as much more. The thought of the long hours they spent across from each other, sparring playfully at first, then lovingly, brought a smile to her lips.

5

With her departure and Ryan's injury, the unit was temporarily being led by crusty veteran detective Callum Reid. The team included Detectives Alan Trembley and Marjorie Pointer. Detective Gaylene Parker from Vice was even called in occasionally for support when things got especially hairy. They were still the most celebrated investigative squad in the department, but without Ryan and Jessie, HSS had lost a bit of its luster.

Jessie stepped over to the poster on the wall and gave herself a quick going-over in its reflection. She looked reasonably professional considering the day and hour. Her shoulder-length brown hair was loose but tidy. Her green eyes were well-rested, which she suspected would change once Ryan came home. She'd been able to maintain her trim, athletic figure through the recent injuries, though she knew she wasn't back in tip-top shape yet.

"Come in," Decker called out, drawing her back into the moment.

Jessie opened the door. She wasn't surprised to find the captain standing up, dressed in the same attire he wore on a weekday afternoon—a jacket, tie, and starched dress shirt. She couldn't tell how long he'd been awake because he looked perpetually worn out, with wrinkles near his eyes and bags under them. The few hairs on his head looked tired and wilted. Even his body, with its concave chest, seemed to fold in on itself. Despite all that, he appeared alert. Tall and skinny, his posture was painfully erect, highlighting his sharp nose and beady eagle eyes, which missed nothing.

"Thanks for making the time, Hunt," he said, gesturing for her to take one of the weathered chairs opposite his desk. "How are you feeling?"

"Tired, Captain. Very tired."

"I'm not surprised to hear that," he replied. "But I meant physically. How's your shoulder? And the burns?"

He was referring to injuries Jessie had suffered before she'd quit the force. Much of her lower back had been badly burned a few months back while rescuing a woman from her burning house, when a man who'd abducted her and then intentionally released her had come back to finish the job. Only weeks later, her left shoulder was dislocated in a life or death struggle with her ex-husband, the same attack in which Ryan had been stabbed and Hannah nearly killed.

"Both are much better," she assured him. "The burns don't hurt anymore, though the doctor says it'll be another year before they heal completely. I'm still in rehab for the shoulder but it doesn't affect me except when I try to get something off the top shelf or do a power lifting session."

"You're very funny, Hunt," Decker said, not laughing. "That should serve you well when Hernandez leaves the hospital. Please let me know what I can do to help. We can have officers stop by to check on him, even just to share war stories. Plus, I know you have security concerns about some of the people you put away reaching out to do harm."

"There are almost too many to keep track of," Jessie conceded.

"If it helps, we've been keeping an extra close eye on former police sergeant Hank Costabile and on Andrea Robinson," Decker said. "You probably heard that Costabile was just sentenced to seven years in prison. And Robinson is still safely incarcerated in a psychiatric prison ward."

"Always reassuring to know the folks who most want to kill me are being physically prevented from doing so, at least for now."

"We can have units do extra patrols by your place, if it sets your mind at ease," Decker offered.

"Thanks, Captain," Jessie replied. "I might take you up on having folks stop by to hang out with Ryan. But I think we're good on security for now. One good thing about inheriting the home of the most celebrated criminal profiler on the West Coast in the last quarter century is that it comes ready-made with elaborate security. I'm still familiarizing myself with everything he had installed. But I'm pretty sure we're set, even in the event of The Purge."

"Well, let me know if you change your mind," he said, either unaware of or unamused by the reference. "We want Hernandez back and anything we can do to expedite that, we will. In the meantime, shall I tell you about the case?"

"Please."

He sat down at his desk and folded his hands.

"Details are still sketchy for reasons that will become clear," he said. "But Millicent Estrada, forty-two, was found dead a few hours ago at a huge party in Holmby Hills. Her neck was broken."

"Should I know who that is?" Jessie asked.

"Not necessarily. She was a well-regarded attorney, one of those 'lawyer to the stars' types. She and her husband, Beto, are both partners in the same firm, which handles everything from contracts to civil cases to criminal defense work. He does a lot of the civil stuff. She specialized in keeping clients off the police blotter and out of jail. They were considered a real power couple until about six months ago, when they announced they were divorcing."

"Ouch," Jessie said. "That sounds awkward."

"Not as much as you might think," Decker corrected. "I've heard that it was fairly amicable. They still worked together. But they've taken very different social paths since the split. He's a homebody and she…let's just say she's spread her wings since they parted ways. That's where it becomes HSS-worthy."

"Pray tell."

Decker tossed her the thin file as he continued.

"Estrada was found at the estate of Jasper Otis."

"The billionaire?" Jessie asked, unable to hide her curiosity.

"Right," Decker confirmed. "And by the way, according to Forbes, it's about fourteen billion."

"Is he a suspect?"

"You'll have to tell me," Decker advised. "The first call reporting the death came in at 3:58 a.m. so it's pretty fresh. I know West L.A. station sent out a detective but I think he might be out of his depth so I snapped it up."

Jessie flipped through the file skeptically.

"This sounds more involved than I think I'm up for right now. I've seen how Jasper Otis operates. The guy runs a media empire and isn't afraid to use it to crush people who get in his way. Do you really want to hand this over to a part-time profiler whose attention is focused on her invalid boyfriend and her rebellious sister?"

"I wouldn't have reached out if I didn't think you were up for it," he told her. "And frankly, I don't have much choice. All my HSS detectives are on other cases right now. You're the only experienced hand at my disposal."

She sensed that he wasn't being completely forthright.

"Captain, is that the only reason?" she pressed.

"Officially, yes," he said, before adding after a brief pause, "Unofficially, I don't trust anyone else on this. Obviously Jasper Otis is an incredibly high-profile person. The pressure on this thing is going to be enormous and I know you can handle it. I also know you can move fast. Once the press gets word of this, it'll be a circus. We have to stay ahead of the news. Do you know anyone more qualified for the job than you are?"

When he laid it out so bluntly, turning the case down felt even harder.

"But you said you don't even have a detective assigned yet?" she asked, incredulous. He really was throwing her to the wolves.

"No. I thought I'd let you pick your partner for this one. Since HSS is a priority unit, I can pull from any station in the city if the need arises. Any detective not currently assigned to a case is yours for the taking."

Jessie smiled despite herself.

"I know what you're doing, Captain," she said.

"What's that?" he asked, feigning innocence.

"You're hoping that by telling me I'm the only one who can handle this case and letting me pick who I work with, you'll make it too tempting for me to say no."

He shrugged noncommittally.

"That's a scurrilous accusation," he said mildly. "Did it work?"

She sighed. It *was* tempting. Her class didn't start until next week. Hannah would be back in school tomorrow. If need be, she could have the nurse work full-time for a few days. And if things got too time-consuming, she could beg off and leave the case in the hands of someone she trusted.

"Two conditions," she said.

"Go ahead."

"First, I have to be home to take care of my family. That means normal hours—no running out in the middle of the night. Second, if it gets to be too much, I can bail without consequence. You can keep the detective for continuity but I'm not putting my home life on the back burner for any case, even one involving a billionaire. Deal?"

Decker scrunched up his face and she thought he was about to balk.

"What detective do you want?"

CHAPTER TWO

"Hello?" Detective Karen Bray said sleepily.

"Karen, it's Jessie Hunt. Sorry to call so early but I need your help."

"What time is it?"

"Six thirty."

"Are you okay, Jessie?" she asked, sounding more alert.

"Yes. But I'm consulting on a time-sensitive case. Captain Decker gave me carte blanche to pick a case partner from any LAPD station and I thought of you."

"What's the case?" Karen asked. Jessie could tell the detective was fully alert now.

"I'll fill you in on the way. Meet me at Hollywood Station right away. We can carpool from there."

"Where are we going?"

"Holmby Hills," Jessie told her. "So put on your nicest work slacks."

Less than thirty minutes later, the two of them were driving west, approaching one of the most expensive pieces of real estate in Los Angeles. Jessie had left her car at Hollywood Station and let Bray drive. It only made sense considering how well her new partner knew the area.

Jessie had only worked with Karen Bray once before but it had been a positive experience. Barely a month ago, the Hollywood detective had been instrumental in helping Jessie and Detective Trembley, who were based out of downtown L.A., steer their way through the murky world of studio politics while investigating the death of an actress on a film shoot.

Jessie remembered Bray saying that she used to work at West L.A. station, which had jurisdiction over the tony Holmby Hills neighborhood. For a case involving someone this rich in an area of town she'd didn't know well, it made perfect sense to partner with a cop she respected who also knew the lay of the land.

It was already paying dividends. As Bray followed the winding curves of Sunset Boulevard, she pointed out various landmarks. There was the Beverly Hills Hotel on their right, with its famed Polo Lounge restaurant. They skirted the northern edge of the Los Angeles Country Club, a popular hangout for the rich and famous. She noted the Playboy Mansion, perhaps the most famous residence in Holmby Hills, though it was far from the most ostentatious.

"That title belongs to The Manor," Bray said, sounding more like a tour guide than a detective. "It's the former home of the late television producer Aaron Spelling. With over a hundred rooms and more than twenty-five bathrooms, it's the largest home in Los Angeles County."

"Why do I get the sense that you've given out-of-town family members this speech more than once?" Jessie asked.

"Is it that obvious?" Bray replied, then continued without waiting for an answer, intentionally using her best narrator voice. "By comparison, the Otis Estate is relatively modest. It has a mere forty-six rooms with nine bedrooms and twelve bathrooms. Otis bought it in 2015 for thirty-three million dollars."

"How do you know all this?" Jessie asked.

Karen smiled sheepishly.

"I read it on Wikipedia while you came over to meet me."

"Did you do a deep dive on Otis too?" Jessie asked.

"Yes, but I didn't really need to. That guy's more ubiquitous than most actual celebrities. Fifty-one years old. Self-made billionaire, media mogul who started one news network, was forced out, and started a new one out of spite. Has a mini-studio that makes half a dozen movies a year. Owns eleven newspapers and multiple high-profile websites, including the major source of gossip on the web. Has an amusement park and resort in Georgia and another one under construction in Oklahoma. Has two planes, a yacht, and the entire floor of an Upper West Side apartment building. And maybe most relevant for our purposes, is a twice divorced bachelor who likes models and actresses and regularly throws parties at his place for hundreds of people. He had one last night."

"Sounds like the kind of fella who will be more than happy to open his home to some nosy investigators," Jessie said sarcastically.

"We're about to find out," Karen replied. "We're here."

They had pulled up to an iron gate. The driveway behind it twisted back a good seventy-five yards before disappearing behind a grove of trees. The actual house was too far back to be seen.

"Should I try the buzzer?" Karen asked.

11

"May as well," Jessie said. "They can't be surprised we're here. I assume cops have been coming and going for hours."

Karen had to get out of the car and walk over to the intercom system, which was about five and half feet high, almost as tall as she was. She pushed the button.

"Estate. How may I assist?" asked an officious male voice.

She held up her badge and ID for the cameras next to the speaker.

"Detective Karen Bray, LAPD, along with criminal profiler Jessie Hunt. We're part of the investigative team."

There was a brief silence before the voice returned.

"Proceed up the drive to the roundabout. Please park in the staff lot to the left of the main house. Someone will meet you."

"I guess we're considered staff now," Jessie said when Karen got back in the car.

"Get used to it," Karen replied as the huge gates slowly opened. "Folks in this neighborhood have treated the police as their personal errand boys for years. It's one of the reasons I left. I got tired of having to kowtow to people just because of their bank accounts."

Jessie said nothing but silently decided that this gave her more reason to like Karen Bray. Anyone who chafed at the arrogance of the powerful got a point in her book. They drove up the driveway, passing the grove, until the house came into view.

It was more of a compound, to be accurate. From what Jessie could tell, it had three distinct sections with connecting passages that together formed a sharp-edged "U," with the most impressive section in front. Designed in the style of a French country palace, it was three stories tall while the side sections were only two. As they pulled up, Jessie could see that off to the right were tennis courts and a greenhouse. To the left, she saw a pool and an adjoining pool house. She could see the edges of other structures that she guessed were cabanas or small guest houses.

They parked in the assigned lot, between a black-and-white and a coroner's van. They had just gotten out when a cute, petite young woman approached them with a clipboard. She wore a white tennis skirt and a short-sleeved royal blue collared shirt monogrammed with the cursive letters "*JO*." She gave a perfunctory smile before launching in.

"Hello, I'm Matilda, part of Jasper's Estate Team. I'm here as your guide. I'll be taking you to join your colleagues. But before we enter the house, I need you both to sign these NDAs, please."

Jessie and Karen exchanged surprised, mildly amused looks.

"We're law enforcement professionals," Karen said slowly. "We don't sign non-disclosure agreements with private citizens."

"Oh, don't worry," Matilda said as if this was just a misunderstanding. "It's not for anything related to the unfortunate tragedy. It's merely to confirm that you won't reveal or discuss anything or anyone you might see on the premises that would infringe on Jasper's privacy or possessions or the privacy of his guests."

"Is that all?" Jessie asked acidly.

"Yes," Matilda replied, not picking up on the sarcasm.

"In that case," Jessie announced, "we're law enforcement professionals. We don't sign non-disclosure agreements with private citizens."

"But your colleagues all signed without a problem," Matilda protested, holding out the clipboard beseechingly.

"That's actually a big problem...for them," Karen said. "Now, please stop shoving those papers in our face and take us to the crime scene."

Matilda, crestfallen, lowered the clipboard.

"Hey," Jessie said in her best buck-up voice. "If your boss gives you a hard time about this, tell him we threatened to arrest you. But for now, we need to see that body, so let's get moving."

Matilda nodded and turned, motioning for them to follow. She led them through the grand foyer of the central section, or as Matilda called it, the South House. They passed an imposing spiral staircase that coiled up all three stories. Behind it was glassed-in elevator.

"The incident occurred in West House, in Jasper's personal wing," Matilda said as she scurried along.

"Personal wing?" Karen repeated.

"Yes. The estate has three sections—East House, South House, and West House. East House is mostly for business. South House is for entertaining. And West House is the residential section. There are several wings within West House, including Jasper's personal wing. It includes his sitting room, his game room, his entertainment room, his private dining room, his bedroom, and his bathroom. That's where the victim was found."

She led them through a hallway that connected the South and West "Houses" and then along a winding corridor, until they reached a wide stairwell. The corridor continued further along the first floor, leading to some floor-to-ceiling plastic sheeting outside another door at the end.

But Matilda stopped here and jogged up the stairs with a vigor that made Karen roll her eyes at Jessie.

Their guide may have been young and full of boundless energy, but not everyone else was. Karen's seen-it-all reaction reminded Jessie of their first meeting at Sovereign Studios, when the detective's blouse was smudged with paint from her second grader's science project. Her top was unsullied today but she still had that harried mom vibe. In her late thirties, with thin, brittle-looking dirty blonde hair and exhausted gray eyes, she was in solid shape but clearly didn't have any interest in ascending the stairs at anything more than a steady pace.

Jessie might have been almost a decade younger and more athletic, but she was on the same wavelength. She brought up the rear as they made their way to the second floor. She was almost to the top when she felt her phone buzz.

She took it out to find a message from Hannah, who must have just woken up. There was no "hello" or "good morning." Instead it simply said, "You better be back before Ryan gets here. I can't do that on my own."

Jessie responded with a thumbs-up emoji. There was no way she wasn't going to be there for him when he came through that door. This case might be important but it wasn't even close to her top priority today.

Matilda pushed open two heavy doors and led them along the thickly carpeted, art-adorned second floor corridor.

"This is Jasper's wing," she said in a respectful, hushed voice as they passed through the corridor into what Jessie guessed was the entertainment room, which had a pool table, a foosball table, a ping-pong table, and several old-style stand-up video game machines along with a pinball machine. A gigantic TV monitor, which covered an entire wall, stood in front of two couches and an easy chair. It looked like ten people could comfortably watch whatever he put on.

Matilda walked obliviously through the room, then through the sitting room until she reached a pair of ornate mahogany doors, one of which was ajar. She pushed it open all the way and stepped to the side so Jessie and Karen could enter. When they did, they finally found the folks they'd been looking for.

Four uniformed cops were milling about. There was a woman in a crime scene unit jacket standing with a man in a suit, who was leaning just outside a door Jessie assumed led to the bathroom. He was in his late forties, with unkempt black hair and a paunch that threatened to burst the buttons on his dress shirt.

"That's Ernie Purcell," Karen said, nodding at the man in the suit. "He was likely the assigned detective before HSS pulled rank. I doubt he'll be psyched about it."

"Why is that?" Jessie asked.

"Ernie's kind of territorial," she warned. "He's also a bit of a toady. If he's on this case, it means the higher-ups want it resolved quickly and cleanly."

"So you're a big fan then?" Jessie mused.

"I don't like to speak ill of anyone. But he's going to be an impediment to doing this the right way."

"Good to know," Jessie said as she crossed the enormous bedroom, glancing out the floor to ceiling windows, past the balcony to the expansive lawn below. In the distance she saw a large garden with a hedge maze and what she thought might be enclosures for a petting zoo.

Ernie Purcell looked up with a scowl etched on his face. In that moment Jessie decided that the best way to deal with this guy was to get him back on his heels. If he felt in control, it would be that much harder for her to get the information she needed. She wanted him unsettled, even if that required a little creative storytelling.

"Who're you?" he demanded unsociably.

"Ernie," she said when she got to him. "You're hurting my feelings here. Are you telling me you don't remember we met at the True Blue Gala last year? You were so friendly back then, some girls might say too friendly. And now you're acting all standoffish. What's a gal to think?"

"I didn't go to the gala last year," he said flatly.

"Wow," Jessie said, getting into the spirit of the lie. "You must have really knocked back quite a few to have forgotten our time together. I'll try not to take offense. Maybe you can make it up to me by giving us the lowdown."

"Lady, I don't know who you are…" he started before Karen cut him off.

"Sure you do, Ernie," she said. "You might not remember the gala. But I saw your eyes when Ms. Hunt walked over. You recognize her from being on your old boob tube. There's not a cop in this city who isn't familiar with the exploits of Jessie Hunt, so you can quit pretending. Moreover, if she's here, you know why. You're just upset that you've been relegated to the second team."

If it was possible, Purcell's scowl got even more pronounced.

"Not great to see you, Bray," he muttered. "I thought we were rid of you for good. And I'm nobody's second teamer."

"Look," Jessie said amiably, as she put on her gloves. "I don't want to get into a pissing contest with you, Ernie. I'm sure you've done a bang-up job so far. But Detective Bray is right. HSS has claimed this case. And as the assigned HSS primary, I've tasked Bray with being my partner on this case. Your assistance is appreciated. In fact, it's required. But you will be in a secondary role. So why don't you start filling your role and update us on what you have so far. Shall we check out the scene?"

For a second Purcell looked like he might balk. But then he looked at Jessie, with her gloves on, and a nasty smile came over his face.

"By all means, Ms. Hunt," he said with fake politeness, "let's."

He extended his hands as if to welcome her into the bathroom. Unsure of the reason for the sudden change of heart, she stepped inside, with Karen right behind her. The second she looked around, her heart sank.

The bathroom looked immaculate. And there was no dead body in it.

CHAPTER THREE

"Where the hell is the victim?" she demanded.

"I'm surprised you didn't pass her on your way up here," Purcell replied with barely contained malice. "She was taken out in a body bag ten minutes ago."

"How could you let that happen?" Karen demanded. "This is a crime scene. It should have taken hours to properly document and clear it."

"I couldn't wait hours," someone behind them said.

Both women stepped out of the bathroom to find themselves face to face with Jasper Otis. Jessie managed to keep her expression from changing, but only due to years of hiding her emotions from killers. Karen was slightly less successful as she gasped slightly at the sight of him.

Jasper Otis wasn't an especially imposing-looking man. He was of average build—around five foot ten and 175 pounds. He had shaved off what was left of his thinning grayish-brown hair and wore glasses with lenses so thin, Jessie wondered if they were for show. He was tan, but not overly so. He was in good shape, but not so ripped that he looked like he was desperately chasing youth. His eyes were stunningly blue and piercing. They were the feature that pushed him from pleasantly bland into the mildly attractive camp.

"In murder investigations," Jessie said, recovering quickly enough that her reply came naturally, "the homeowner doesn't usually get to make those decisions."

"I'm so sorry," he said convincingly. "My home has never been the scene of a crime before so I guess I didn't know the rules. Just the thought of a dead body in the shower I use every day was so unsettling, I had to do something. So I asked Carlotta and the housekeeping staff to move her to the sitting room. They used gloves and everything so their fingerprints wouldn't get on her."

Jessie said nothing, though her internal alert system was going off. The idea that this guy didn't know any better when it came to preserving a crime scene was laughable. She found herself instantly suspicious of him.

"Mr. Otis," Karen said, now recovered. "You own a movie studio that has made multiple police thrillers. Have you never watched one of them? Are you seriously telling us that you didn't realize that disturbing a crime scene was a problem?"

"No, detective," he replied, his voice warm as honey. "I'm telling you that I freaked out. I'm embarrassed about it. I regret it. Unfortunately, it seems that it's too late to do anything about it. I've created many things in my career but a time machine is not yet among them."

"We have photos," Purcell volunteered, suddenly much less combative now that he was in the presence of Otis. "The coroner will have a preliminary report later today. CSU checked for prints and DNA. We're talking to Mr. Otis's security team about pulling camera footage. Despite the regrettable way this started, I think we've got a lot to work with."

"There you go," Otis said enthusiastically. "Making the most of a situation I screwed up. I wish I could say it was the first time. Anyway, as you might imagine, I've got a full day, so I'm going to leave you in Matilda's capable hands."

"Mr. Otis," Jessie said as he headed toward the mahogany bedroom doors, "we'll need to interview you."

"Of course," he said, not stopping or turning around. "I don't know much but talk to Nancy and she'll put you on my schedule. Until then, the best of luck to you."

He was gone before Jessie could say anything else. She was tempted to chase after him and force him to answer her questions right now. But getting as much detail as possible about the particulars of the crime seemed like a higher priority. She sighed.

"Who's Nancy?" Karen asked.

"Nancy Salter, she's the estate manager," Matilda said. "She runs the day-to-day operations here. She also coordinates Jasper's schedule, in conjunction with Rune, of course, when he's working from home."

"Who's Rune?" Jessie asked.

"Rune Barbato is Jasper's executive assistant. He's in charge of Jasper's day-to-day when he's off estate. But on estate days like today, he defers to Nancy."

"Sounds complicated," Jessie noted.

"Not once you get used to it," Matilda insisted. "I'll make sure to reach out to Nancy to have her pencil you in for some talk time with Jasper."

Jessie was tempted to ask if "talk time" was a Jasper Otis invention but felt herself slipping down the rabbit hole and changed tacks.

"Who examined the body?" she asked Purcell.

"Len Fustos," he said. "He was escorting her out to the van. I think they were getting ready to head out to the morgue."

"Detective Purcell," Jessie began, hoping to appeal to his professionalism by using his title. "Can you please reach out and ask him to come back? We'd like to talk to him before he leaves."

Unable to think of a reason not to, he nodded and pulled out his radio. While they waited, Jessie again caught sight of the woman in the CSU jacket.

"What's your name?" she asked the woman, who looked to be in her late twenties.

"Jan Thomas," she said.

"Did you pull prints and swab?"

Jan nodded.

"What can you tell us?"

"My supervisor is headed back to the lab to test. But preliminary signs weren't promising. No obvious fingerprints. DNA might be another story. But it looked like the perpetrator turned on the shower. Her clothes were soaking wet, at least the ones she had on. Hard to know if that was planned but we're worried the water will make getting DNA tough."

"The clothes she had on?" Karen repeated.

"She was topless except for a bra."

"Did it look like she was sexually assaulted?" Karen asked.

"If you don't mind, Detective," Thomas said, "I'd rather leave that determination to the M.E."

Just then, an older man, likely in his sixties, walked in. He was wearing corduroy slacks, a denim shirt, and sneakers. His glasses were thick and he had thinning, brown hair. He didn't look happy to be there.

"What's the problem?" he demanded.

"Len," Purcell said, "you might remember Detective Karen Bray. She's at Hollywood station now. And this is Jessie Hunt, profiler extraordinaire. They're taking over primary on the case for HSS and they wanted to get your preliminary thoughts before you go to the morgue."

Len frowned, clearly irked that he was being asked for updates when he was so close to being out the door. He seemed about to say something to that effect when Jessie gave him her patented "don't mess

19

with me" stare, the one she'd developed when trying to talk down murderers. An impatient forensic bureaucrat in corduroy pants wasn't going to intimidate her. Apparently it worked, because he started listing information off.

"This is all preliminary, mind you. I won't even have the first draft of the report until tomorrow. But her neck was broken. There were some defensive wounds but only bruising. No cuts or scratches, meaning it'll be harder to get DNA. She had on a bra but was shirtless. Her top was found beside the bed over there in good shape—not ripped, no buttons popped off. She was wet—body and clothing, almost as if she'd been intentionally hosed down. The guy who found her said there was still water on her skin. It hadn't had time to evaporate. She was really drenched. I'm skeptical that we'll find anything usable."

"Any sign of sexual assault?" Karen asked.

"We'll do more comprehensive testing on that when we get back. But initial inspection suggests no."

"That makes sense," Jessie added. "If the perpetrator knew enough to douse her in water to get rid of DNA evidence, and had raped her, he'd likely have removed all her clothes to soak her everywhere. Let's go back to the neck. How pronounced was the break?"

"I mean, it was enough to kill her," Fustos replied.

"I get that, but could you determine the force used? That might be able to tell us how strong the killer is."

"Again, preliminary, but her skull was bobbing like a rag doll. Whoever did this was likely some combination of extremely strong, extremely angry, and/or extremely knowledgeable about how to break a human neck."

Everyone was quiet for a few seconds after that. In that moment, Jessie thought about Jasper Otis, and wondered whether he was might be capable of such brutality. Considering what she knew people to be capable of, it didn't seem like a stretch. Len Fustos finally broke the silence.

"If you'll let me leave," he said irritably, "I can try to get more definitive answers to some of these questions."

Jessie nodded her acquiescence. That was all he needed to disappear from sight.

"So I guess we're at an impasse," Purcell said, trying to co-opt Fustos's attitude.

Karen looked at him like she thought he might be kidding.

"Not quite," she said. "I think we'd like to talk to the guy who found her. Got a name?"

"Sure," he said. "But I don't know that he'll be of much use."

"Why is that?" Jessie asked.

"When we spoke earlier he was so drunk or high or both that it was hard to get a coherent sentence out of him. He was also flipping out a little because of the whole 'finding a dead body' thing."

"Well, maybe he's sobered up a little in the interim," Jessie suggested. "Do you have his address?"

"Yeah, but you won't need it," he said.

"Why not?" Jessie asked.

"Because unless something has changed, he's about five hundred yards from here, passed out in a guest house."

CHAPTER FOUR

Cord Mahoney looked dead.

Apart from the slight whistle he made as he exhaled, there was no visible indication that he was any better off than Millicent Estrada. His body was stiff. His skin was waxy and because he was under the covers, there was no sign of his chest rising and falling. Jessie decided to make sure.

"Wake up, Cord!"

He shot bolt upright, flailing around wildly as he lost his balance and toppled off the valentine-shaped bed. Karen put her hand over her mouth to stifle a giggle. Detective Purcell scowled at her, and Matilda gasped softly. While they all waited for him to gather his wits, Jessie again marveled at the style of the guest house.

It had the look of a fairy tale cottage on the outside, complete with stucco exterior, a faux thatched wooden roof, and colorfully painted bricks around the window frames. But the wooden sign on the door reading "Love Shack" tipped her off that the inside might be a different story. The small living area was decorated with a bright pink leather couch. The walls were covered in photo stills that appeared to be from 1970s-era porn films.

The bedroom where they found Cord was barely large enough for the king bed, shaped like a candy heart. Every wall, along with the ceiling, was mirrored. Jessie half-expected to find a key party bowl lying around.

Cord managed to orient himself and sit on the edge of the bed. His head was in his hands, which rested on his thighs. He looked like he was fighting off nausea.

"How are you doing, Cord?" she asked gently.

He looked up at her and she knew the answer was: not well. While it was obvious that under normal circumstances, he was an attractive guy, these were not normal circumstances. His eyes were more red than hazel. His skin looked pasty. There was sweat on his forehead, where his longish blond hair adhered. Jessie guessed that he was in his early thirties but it was clear that he lived hard so he might actually be a half decade younger than that.

22

"I've been better," he admitted, his voice thick with exhaustion.

"Well, maybe getting some fresh air will help," she suggested. "I saw a picnic table out front. We can talk outside and if you feel like vomiting, the grass is right there. Better that than messing up this...lovely bedroom."

"Who are you again?" he asked.

"I'm Jessie Hunt. I work with the police. This is Detective Karen Bray. You might remember Detective Purcell from earlier. We need to ask you some questions."

He nodded silently and followed them out to the patio table, making sure to sit in the most shaded chair. Jessie, Karen, and Ernie Purcell took the other seats. Matilda stood silently off to the side.

"So," Karen began, "we know you gave Detective Purcell here a statement a few hours ago. But frankly, Cord, it was pretty incoherent. We were hoping you could clear a few things up for us."

"I'll try."

"Great. So why were you in Jasper's personal wing in the first place?"

Jessie didn't mind Karen taking the lead in the interrogation. It actually afforded her the chance to study Cord's body language before diving in herself.

"I had to pee," he said. "But every bathroom was being used."

"Aren't there a dozen of them?" Karen pressed.

"There are a lot," he replied. "But the party was so massive that there were just too many people. Lines to get in were five, six deep. And they were moving slowly, if you know what I mean."

"I don't," Karen said.

Cord glanced over at Matilda as if seeking her permission, but she showed no visible reaction, so he continued.

"Jasper's parties can get wild. Sometimes people in the restrooms are having sex or...doing drugs. They lose track of time. Meanwhile, the rest of us are outside waiting to relieve ourselves."

"But you knew where to find an unoccupied one," Karen prodded.

"Right," he said, getting back on track. "Jasper's been letting me crash here for the last couple of weeks. I work as a VP of production at his studio, Otis Ocular. My condo complex had a gas leak. We were all relocated to a crappy motel. When he found out, he said I could stay here until it got resolved. So we'd hang out sometimes in his wing— play pool, watch a movie. So when things got tight last night, I thought I'd use his private bathroom. No one's supposed to go in the wing

23

without express permission, which is why I thought it might be free. But I also felt guilty because it was like I was betraying his trust."

"Sure," Karen said. "So that's when you found Millicent Estrada. Did you recognize her?"

"Not then, because I was so freaked out and she looked so messed up, with her neck and all. But later on, when I saw a picture of how she usually looks, she was familiar. I think she's some kind of lawyer or something. And she'd gone to lots of Jasper's parties lately. I'd see her at the ones with fifty people and the ones with five hundred. But I didn't really know her, if that's what you're asking."

"So she was a regular at the parties?" Jessie clarified.

He shrugged.

"I couldn't really say what makes for a regular. Jasper throws so many of them and there are always tons of people coming and going, doing all kinds of wild stuff. It's usually a madhouse. But I've definitely seen her around."

"And she was wet when you found her?" Jessie reconfirmed.

"Yeah, when I shook her, hoping she'd wake up, water was dripping off her."

Karen leaned in and Jessie could sense that she was about to get more aggressive.

"Cord, Detective Purcell here says you were pretty out of it when you gave your statement earlier. Is that correct?"

"Yeah, I'd been partying pretty hard."

"In light of that, is it possible that you inadvertently stumbled upon Ms. Estrada alive in Mr. Otis's personal wing and mistook her for a threat of some kind? Maybe lashed out at what you thought was an attacker?"

Cord looked at her as if she was crazy.

"No way," he insisted firmly. "I was messed up, sure. But I didn't do anything like that. I walked into that bathroom and saw her in the shower. I tried to help but she was already dead. I admit I was high out of my mind. But I didn't touch that chick. Give me a lie detector test. I've done some things I'm not proud of in my life, maybe even illegal things, but not this."

And then, as if the stress of asserting his innocence had caught up to him, he suddenly leaned over to the side and vomited in the grass.

As Jessie looked at the guy, sickly and pathetic, she internally dismissed him as a suspect. Not because he might not be capable of doing something awful in a drunken stupor, but because she doubted he

24

could keep it hidden. If he was guilty, Cord Mahoney would have already confessed by now.

"Thanks for thinking of coming out here," he said to Jessie appreciatively when he'd caught his breath.

"Sure thing, Cord," she said before turning her attention back to the others, Matilda in particular. "This is a waste of time. We need to talk to the person who actually runs this place. That's the estate manager. Take us to Nancy Salter now, please."

CHAPTER FIVE

They left Cord to sleep it off in his valentine bed.

Matilda led them to meet with Nancy Salter, who was supposedly going to get them in to formally interview Jasper Otis. As they followed the young girl, zipping past multiple guest houses at breakneck speed, Jessie and Karen considered what they'd just seen.

"I know they took Cord's prints and DNA, but I doubt it's going to turn up much," Jessie said resignedly.

"You don't think it could be him?" Karen asked.

"Never say never," Jessie replied. "I've been burned too often to make that mistake. But it doesn't make a lot of sense to me. That whole wing was unoccupied. If he'd killed her, he could have walked right out of there and back to the party and no one would have been the wiser. But he called nine-one-one, gave his name, and stuck around, even though he was under the influence. Plus, even though polygraphs aren't infallible, the general public doesn't know that. Volunteering to take one suggests he's either confident of his innocence or a sociopath of epic proportions. He didn't strike me as the latter."

Karen was about to respond when her phone rang. The way her face fell when she saw the caller and slowed her pace, Jessie knew this wasn't going to be pleasant. She pretended not to notice and walked ahead, joining Purcell.

"Can you send me those crime scene photos?" she asked him. "I don't want to wait for the preliminary report tomorrow to look at the body for the first time."

He nodded without speaking and pulled out his own phone. Behind them Jessie could hear part of Karen's conversation.

"I take him almost every week," she said testily. "How hard is it for you to cut up some orange slices, sit on a lawn chair while cheering occasionally, then hand out said orange slices?"

Whatever the person on the other end of the line said, it didn't go over well.

"I'm terribly sorry that you'll have to miss the Rams game. Maybe you can record it. And if not, they play about fourteen more this year, so I think you'll get over it."

26

They were approaching a severe-looking woman standing on a stone staircase overlooking the garden and hedge maze. Jessie got the distinct suspicion that it was Nancy Salter and glanced back at Karen, giving her the official "time to wrap it up" look. Karen nodded.

"Just make it work," she said. "We all have burdens. You have to find his cleats. I have to go solve a murder. Goodbye."

Karen hung up just as they came to a stop. Jessie glanced over at Ernie Purcell. To his credit, he gave no indication that he'd heard a word of the conversation.

"Detectives," Matilda said, "this is Nancy Salter. She's the estate manager for Otis Estate. Nancy, you already know Detective Purcell. This is Detective Karen Bray and Jessie Hunt, a criminal profiler."

Nancy Salter looked formidable. She appeared to be in her late forties. She was tall, even looking down at Jessie, who was five foot ten. Her coal black hair was tied up in a tight bun that made her already pinched face look like a raisin. She wore no obvious makeup but had on an elaborate business suit, complete with a doily-style scarf that made Jessie wonder if she'd walked into an episode of *Downton Abbey*.

"Hello," Nancy Salter said, her voice both loud and nasally. "We're pleased to have you. I've scheduled a ten thirty a.m. meeting with Jasper to discuss what he's able to share regarding the matter in question. In the meantime, I've collected some of the revelers from last night's festivities that are still on the property. If you wish to interview them, I'll take them to you now."

She began walking without waiting for permission.

"How many people are we talking about?" Karen asked as they all rushed to keep up.

"About two dozen, I'd say."

"We're going to need the names of everyone who attended the party last night," Karen said.

Nancy Salter looked back at her and seemed on the verge of laughing, but managed to contain it.

"I'm afraid that's quite impossible," she said.

"Why?" Karen pressed.

"Because there was no guest list. Jasper is very welcoming. He invites friends and expects them to invite people he might find interesting. I can probably write down the names of people I'm certain were here, but that will be a mere fraction of the total actual attendees. To be honest, I wish Jasper would be a little more formal when it comes to his gatherings. It's quite difficult to ensure we have enough

27

food and beverages when, on any given night, we don't know whether to expect twenty visitors or two hundred. I can tell you that based on the caterer's bill, I estimate there were between four hundred fifty and six hundred people here last night."

Jessie decided to pursue a different area of inquiry.

"I noticed cameras all over the property. Has your security team handed that footage over to Detective Purcell yet?"

"They're collecting what's available as we speak," Salter assured her.

"Great," Jessie said. "I'd like them to especially focus on the personal wing, from six p.m. until the first officers arrived on the scene."

Nancy Salter did actually laugh at that one.

"Forgive my impertinence," she said quickly. "It's just that the notion that Jasper would allow his private residence to be monitored is laughable."

"But I saw cameras there as well," Jessie said, trying not to get annoyed by the woman's attitude.

"Yes, they were installed in plain view as a deterrent. But they're inactive. In fact, the residential wing and the garden hedge maze we just left are the only areas on the entire estate where there is no monitoring allowed."

"Why the hedge maze?" Karen wondered.

"Jasper enjoys spending time there. It's a place of solitude and mystery that relaxes him. And since he values his privacy, of course he wouldn't want cameras there any more than in his own bedroom."

"Ms. Salter," Jessie said, "I have to say, I find the assertion that, in the home of a public figure like Mr. Otis, in the middle of a massive party, with all the security on this property, there is no footage at all in the area where the crime took place…hard to buy."

Salter stared at her with what Jessie suspected was her most severe expression, the one she saved for employees who'd failed her or her boss. Jessie stared back, undaunted, waiting for an answer.

"Ms. Hunt, all I can tell you is our policy. I'm sorry that it doesn't comport with your expectations, but there's nothing I can do about that. What I *can* do is leave you in Matilda's care to conduct any guest interviews you choose to do while I reconfirm your meeting with Jasper and attend to other errands."

"I assumed you'd be staying with us," Karen said.

28

"You assumed incorrectly, Detective Bray. My duties are numerous on this Sunday morning. Keeping Otis Estate running is much like operating an unconventional business. Jasper has a new personal chef who I need to check in on. The gardening staff is in an uproar over the trampling of several rose bushes last night. We are trying to resolve a mold issue in one residential wing of West House. And someone appears to have released one of the goats from the petting zoo and dressed another in a tube top. So I'll have to take my leave of you. But rest assured, I will collect you when it's time to chat with Jasper. Be well."

She was gone before anyone could reply. Matilda stepped forward.

"Would you like to speak to the guests now?" she asked.

Jessie, Karen, and Purcell shared an exasperated look.

"Sure," Karen finally relented.

"Ernie," Jessie said as they followed Matilda. "I know what Salter said, but have whoever's collecting the video footage from last night check the residence just in case."

He nodded and pulled out his phone to text someone. She was tempted to see if he'd really made the request but decided she had to give the guy some autonomy, even if she was inclined to believe Karen's assertion that he'd be more of a hindrance than a help.

As they made their way to the pool, where the assembled guests waited, Jessie could have sworn she saw a goat trotting behind a distant bush.

CHAPTER SIX

The guests were mostly useless.

Few had much recollection of where they were at any point during the night.

"Can you tell me where it is?" one still-drunk girl wondered when Jessie asked if she'd ever been in Jasper's personal wing. "I'd love to check it out."

"Jasper's awesome," a swarthy guy smoking a clove cigarette told them. "Coolest dude ever."

"That's not what I asked," Karen reminded him. "I want to know if you've been to his personal wing?"

"He has a personal wing? That's so cool!"

They gave up on him and tried to question a group of ultra-fit twenty-something girls in yoga pants who were sipping mimosas at a patio table. None of them knew about the personal wing but several happily name-dropped when asked if they could list any attendees.

"I got Rance Jensen to sign my boob," one offered.

"Me too," another squealed.

"The lead singer of that Hubert Humphrey band or whatever it's called dedicated a song to me when they were playing that acoustic set by the fire pit," said a third.

Jessie suddenly felt old. She'd never even heard of the band. She was also exhausted. After two hours of interviewing mostly still-drunk partiers, she was actually glad when Nancy Salter reappeared at precisely 10:20 to collect them.

"You're relieved, Matilda," she said. "Take your break. I'll escort our guests to see Jasper. Please come to the personal wing momentarily so you can retrieve them upon the completion of their visit."

Matilda nodded and scurried off. Salter led them back along the route they'd followed previously, away from the pool and cabanas, past a series of guest houses, skirting the petting zoo and the hedge maze as they returned to the back entrance of South House.

"Find the missing goat?" Jessie asked.

"We did. Thanks for your concern. Unfortunately, one of our keepers suffered a kick to the shin while retrieving him. He's been sent to the ER with a possible break—just another day in paradise."

It was a testament to Salter's general inscrutability that Jessie couldn't tell if she was being serious or sarcastic. They turned right from South House and again passed the hall connecting it to West House. They were just starting up the stairs when Karen pointed down to the end of the corridor.

"Is that where the mold problem is?" she asked.

"Indeed," Salter replied. "We only just learned of it. Now that whole area has to be closed off while they do the remediation. We're lucky it didn't happen last month when Jasper was hosting a wedding. There were a dozen overnight guests, including four in that wing. We would have had to scramble to find them accommodations. Small blessings, I suppose."

She climbed the stairs even faster than Matilda. Jessie was out of breath trying to keep up. When they arrived at the entrance to Jasper's wing, Salter pressed a button on the intercom.

"Yes," Jasper asked.

"I have our friends from LAPD here to speak with you," Salter replied.

"Please show them in, Nancy," he said.

She led them through the array of rooms until they came to his private dining room. Salter motioned for them to take seats. They did as she moved to the corner of the room, where she remained standing. Moments later Otis arrived, talking on his cell phone.

"Tell them it's my final offer," he said as he took a seat, silently mouthing "sorry" to them. He waited for several seconds before replying, "I expect an answer one way or another by noon tomorrow. Otherwise we'll move on to Belgium."

He hung up without saying goodbye, put the phone in his pocket, and gave them his most charming smile. It felt false to Jessie.

"So," he said, jumping right in. "As I told you earlier, I'm not sure how much help I can be. But I'm here to try. What do you want to know?"

"Where were you last night between three and four in the morning?" Karen asked, launching straight in.

He sat there for a moment with a look of contemplation on his face.

"I couldn't tell you for certain," he said. "I was a bit of a social butterfly, moving from group to group, chatting, making sure everyone

31

was having a good time. There was a period where I went off for a little private time with a lady friend in the pool house. But I think that was earlier, closer to two-ish."

"Would you be willing to let us check your phone so we can verify your movements using GPS?" Karen asked.

He smiled warmly at her.

"I'd be willing but it won't help much. You see, I'm an investor in a company that has developed a new kind of dampening technology. It was so promising that I became an early adopter. It prevents location data from getting delivered. I think it's going to change the world of privacy. Eventually everyone will be able to turn their dampener on or off, depending on whether they want their location known or not. The ability to add it to individual phones isn't there yet. But I had them set up a digital dampening net that covers my entire property. So there's no GPS data to reference."

Jessie seethed silently, unable to believe her ears. The GPS signals didn't work. Neither did some cameras. The crime scene had been interfered with. This guy had guilty written all over him and yet he seemed nothing but cool and calm.

"You do realize that while that may be an exciting technology," Karen said with more diplomacy than Jessie was currently capable of mustering, "it makes it much more challenging to eliminate you as a person of interest."

"An irony I'm now aware of," he noted. "Still, I'm sure that between guest interviews and security footage, you'll find it's easy to keep tabs on me. I was in public spaces for most of the night."

"We'll need the name of your lady friend," Karen said.

"You see, Detective Bray," he said remorsefully, "that's why Matilda asked you to sign the NDA. It wasn't for any nefarious reason, just so no one goes blabbing about my sex life to a competitor. If that's going to get out, I want it to be on Blabber."

Jessie immediately tensed up at the reference.

"What's Blabber?" Purcell asked, speaking for the first time.

Jasper Otis smiled broadly, exposing his brilliant white teeth.

"Normally I'd be offended, Detective," he said. "But considering that you're way outside our preferred demographic, I suppose I should be relieved. Blabber is the highest-trafficked gossip site on the web."

Jessie couldn't help but butt in.

"It's also the website that just recently had scumbags making harassing phone calls to me and showing up to take photos of me entering the building where I used to live."

Otis smiled at her without a hint of remorse.

"The people's right to know cannot be abridged, Ms. Hunt," he said. "Maybe that's why more people visit Blabber on a daily basis than the sites for *The New York Times*, *The Washington Post*, and CNN combined. But setting all that aside, you can see why I'm disinclined to reveal the name of my companion."

"Mr. Otis," Purcell said, "I can assure you that as law enforcement, it's a violation of our oath to reveal information like that, with or without an NDA. Doing so could result in the loss of our jobs."

"And yet you signed yours, Detective," Otis noted.

"I did," Purcell admitted, turning slightly pink. "But my point is that sensitive information is safe with us. It would only come out in a court proceeding under specified circumstances. But if you think it can help establish your alibi, I'd highly recommend you provide the name. It could help exonerate you."

"Besides," Jessie added, "I assume this companion signed an NDA, yes?"

"She did."

"Then, unless there were others with you at the time, the only people who would know about your lady friend are her and the people in this room. If something leaks, it'll be easy to know who to go after. And if we're all being honest here, Mr. Otis, we both know that you're going to leak her name anyway if it helps your image. So there's no real downside."

"Ms. Hunt, how dare you defame my gentlemanly good name," he said in an over-the-top Southern accent which didn't hide the fact that he hadn't consented to share the woman's name.

Jessie decided this was the time, when he seemed to be enjoying himself and had let his guard down slightly, to ask the question that had been on her mind.

"Do you feel bad, sir?"

"Excuse me?"

"Do you feel bad that a woman was murdered in your bathroom, Mr. Otis?"

For the briefest of moments, he seemed thrown. But it was just a flicker in the eyes. Almost as quickly as it had appeared, it was gone.

"Of course I do, Ms. Hunt," he said gravely. "It wasn't just 'a woman.' It was Milly Estrada, a friend, a woman I respected immensely. While she never represented me personally, her firm did. And I have friends who extolled her dedication and her skill. They found her in *my* shower, with her neck broken and no shirt on, hosed down like an animal. I feel more than bad, Ms. Hunt, I feel devastated. And if I don't display that to your satisfaction, I'm sorry. I'm trying to put on a brave face and push through this because lingering on it, thinking about how awful her final moments must have been, well it's too terrible to fathom. Call me a coward but I guess I'm just not up to it."

Nobody spoke for several seconds. Jessie was genuinely unsure whether this was all for show or if Jasper Otis was so used to living on the bright stage that this was really how he comported himself in a moment of grief.

"Do you have any more questions for me?" he asked with hint of an edge in his voice.

She did and was about to ask one when her phone buzzed. She glanced at it and saw that it was from Hannah. It read simply: "Hospital called. Ryan will be here in just over an hour. You need to be here at noon to sign him out."

She looked up. Otis was staring at her expectantly.

"That's all for now," she said, "though we may need to revisit some issues with you later. If you can provide Detective Purcell with your companion's name and contact info, he'll guard it zealously. In the meantime, I offer my condolences on your loss."

She didn't wait for Nancy Salter to open the door for her, or for Matilda, who was waiting outside the dining room, to lead her outside. By the time Karen caught up to her in the parking lot, she was standing impatiently by the passenger door.

"You booked out of there in a hurry," she said. "Everything okay?"

Jessie nodded. She'd explain on the way. For now they had to move.

"How fast can you get back to the station?"

CHAPTER SEVEN

Jessie looked at the time as she pulled up in the driveway of the house. It was 11:53.

When she opened the front door, Hannah was sitting on the couch with her arms crossed and a glower on her face.

"How's it going, sunshine?" Jessie asked.

She already knew the answer. Her sister's green eyes were fiery, her sandy blonde hair was wild, as if she'd started brushing it but then gave up. The way she was folded up into herself, no one would guess she was almost as tall as Jessie.

"You go off to investigate a case on a Sunday morning and leave me with some lame note?"

"I didn't want to interrupt your beauty sleep," Jessie told her.

"And you made me think I might be stuck here alone when Ryan showed up."

"I'm here now," Jessie said, trying not to escalate the situation.

"Just barely," came the surly reply.

Jessie sighed internally.

"How'd you sleep?" she asked.

Hannah looked like she was about to offer more snark, then seemed to reconsider.

"The same as usual, so not well," she admitted. "This time I had the nightmare where our serial killer father murders my adoptive parents. I guess I should be glad. At least it's a change of pace from when your serial killer stalker buddy made me watch while he slaughtered my foster parents."

Jessie walked over to the couch and sat down beside her.

"I'm sorry," she said. "I wish I could tell you when those kinds of dreams will go away. But I'm still waiting for it to happen for me."

Hannah nodded before seeming to brighten.

"Hey," she finally said in a sarcastically chipper tone, "at least when Ryan gets here, we'll be too exhausted and stressed out by our current lives to focus on the past ones, right?"

Before Jessie could respond there was a knock on the door.

"I guess we're about to find out," she said and walked over to open it.

When she did, she found that two hospital staffers and a nurse had already removed Ryan from the ambulance and guided his wheelchair up the ramp to the porch. Her boyfriend looked up at her and, in a slow, labored voice, spoke.

"Would you...like...buy some...Girl Scout Cookies?"

Jessie couldn't help but laugh. He'd probably been working on that the whole way over.

"Come on in," she said after leaning down to give him a kiss.

She bit her lip, trying to keep tears at bay. It had been such a long road. Now he was finally home. The emotion of the moment was almost overwhelming.

The staffers pushed him inside, had Jessie sign some paperwork, and left again. The whole process took about three minutes. The nurse, a blandly pleasant forty-something woman named Patty, remained behind. She was here to help Ryan acclimate to his new surroundings. But when she left this evening, they'd be on their own. Luckily Jessie had contracted with a private nursing company to have folks in the house as needed.

"We'll show you around in a sec but I wanted to give you a moment to settle in," she said, wheeling him over near the couch where Hannah, who hadn't gotten up to greet him, still sat. "Excited to be out?"

Ryan nodded. He opened his mouth but it took several seconds for the words to follow. Each one was an effort.

"I think...they are...excited...that I'm...gone."

"I'm not surprised," Jessie replied. "Everyone knows that your winning charm starts to fade around the six-week mark."

Ryan laughed, though it came out as more of a throaty rasp. As improved as he looked from even a month ago, it was still tough to look at him and not picture the man she used to know. Once muscular and tan, he was now pale and his skin looked pouchy over his flesh. His hair had been cut shorter than usual, almost like a crew cut, for easier maintenance. The one thing that hadn't changed was his deep, brown eyes. They still had the same warmth and intensity as always. But right now they looked troubled.

"What is it?' she asked.

He tried to get his mouth to form the words in his head but it was a struggle.

"Phy...phys...ph..." he seemed to give up on that word and skipped to the next, "therapy."

"Right," Jessie replied, getting what he meant. "The rehabilitative therapist will start tomorrow. That will be every day. Once you've made some progress on the activities of daily living, we'll bring in the physical therapist to help you get your strength and mobility back. But we're going to have to be patient. Remember Dr. Badalia wants you to take it one step at a time. Biting off more than you can chew could be detrimental to your long-term recovery."

Ryan shook his head.

"Not...average...bear," he insisted.

Jessie smiled.

"Don't I know it. So do you want to check out the new digs?" she asked. "Hannah, would you like to do the honors?"

Hannah, who had been silent up to now, nodded.

"Hey, Ryan," she said quietly as she stood and gave him a kiss on the cheek. "Good to have you back. Now I won't have to take the trash out to the curb every week."

Ryan did his raspy laugh. Jessie smiled, glad that at least her sister wasn't taking her frustration out on him. As Jessie and Nurse Patty trailed behind, Hannah wheeled him through the house, pointing out all the added features, including the handrails everywhere, the assist bars to get in the bath and on the toilet, and the call buttons in every room. She also showed him the emergency call button necklace they'd gotten for him. That got a huge grin from him.

"I've fallen...and...I can't...get up," he said.

Hannah looked over at Jessie, confused.

"It's from an old commercial," she said. "Look it up on YouTube."

When they got to Jessie's office, Ryan looked over at her.

"Was Garland's?" he asked.

"Yeah," she said, confirming that this had been the home office of Garland Moses, the man who'd left her this house in his will. The fact that they only lived here now because Garland had been brutally murdered by her ex-husband was something she was still trying to come to terms with.

"Sorry," Ryan croaked, reaching out for her hand and squeezing it tight. He'd actually been the detective who first investigated Garland's murder and the person who had to break the news to her. He knew how much the old guy meant to her, even if he couldn't verbalize it yet.

Hannah started to turn the wheelchair back down the hall when Ryan held up his hand.

"Me," he insisted. "Need to…practice."

Hannah lifted her hands in the air. Ryan nodded his approval, then grabbed the wheels and tried to turn the chair around. But it was a tight fit for the hall, with little room for error. Twice he banged into a wall before attempting to turn it in the other direction. That was even less successful. After three failed attempts, he got frustrated and slammed the chair against the wall.

"Dammit," he yelled, loud and clear.

"Let me help," Jessie said, reaching for the handles on the back of the chair.

"Don't…touch!" he barked.

She yanked her hands back, startled at his anger. Unsure what to do, she looked over at Patty. The nurse, just out of Ryan's line of sight, put her hands in front of her, palms down, and mimed pushing them down, as if to say "let's lower the temperature a bit." Before Jessie could try, Ryan sighed heavily.

"I'm…sorry," he said. "Tired…ornery."

"That okay," she said quickly. "It's already been a huge day. Why don't we take you to the bedroom so you can rest a bit?"

She pushed him down to the master bedroom and, with Patty's assistance, helped him lie down in the new hospital bed. He looked at Jessie.

"You?" he asked. She knew what he meant.

"Dr. Badalia thinks you'll get better sleep if you're in this type of bed, so I'm going to stay in the guest room for a little while, but only until we get back into a normal routine. And I'll still hang out in here to make you watch home renovation shows. Now that I'm stronger than you, I control the remote."

He smiled but she could tell he wasn't happy. She realized that he'd been looking forward to sharing a bed again as much as she had. Unfortunately, no one had thought to tell him that bit of normalcy would be delayed a while longer. Still, he put on a brave face.

"Good," he said. "You…snore."

Once they'd closed the door, the three women retreated to the breakfast table. Jessie tried to ignore the ache she felt in her chest at having Ryan here, but still not truly with her.

"Patty, are you sure you're cool sticking around for a while longer?" she asked.

"Not a problem. I'm contracted through the afternoon. Besides, for the first day, it's always helpful to have a pro around to navigate personal care issues."

"Awesome," Hannah said, "because I was thinking of going over to Melrose to liven up my wardrobe."

Jessie looked at her sternly.

"Did you mean 'may I please go to Melrose to look for clothes'?" she asked.

"Yeah, that."

"You may go for two hours," Jessie said. "I need to do some research on this case and it might require some driving around. I don't want to leave Patty alone to handle everything on Ryan's first day back. Got it?"

"Got it," Hannah snapped.

"I mean it," Jessie reiterated. "You need to be back inside the house by two p.m. or future wardrobe-livening sessions will be put in jeopardy."

"Don't worry," Hannah said, hopping up and grabbing her purse. "I'm very responsible for my age."

She was out the door before Jessie could come up with the response she wanted, which would have involved reminding her sister of the myriad times she'd proven that claim wasn't true. It was probably for the best.

Once Hannah was gone, Jessie retreated to her office. She settled in to try to wrap her head around the case, as she imagined Garland had done so often in this very spot. She glanced at the painting on the wall that hid Garland's safe. She already knew that it only held one thing. Inside was a fireproof lockbox that contained all the material, both paper and digital, on just one case: The Night Hunter.

That was the serial killer who had apparently haunted Garland until his death. Even though the man was believed to have died decades ago in an altercation that almost killed Garland, it was clear that her mentor still had his doubts. Otherwise, why would he have saved every scrap of information on the man and his crimes?

Jessie shook her head in frustration. It served no purpose to think about a serial killer last seen in the prior century. There was a murder just hours ago that she'd been tasked to solve. That's where she needed to keep her focus, so that's where she fixed it. She studied the crime scene photos that Ernie Purcell had texted her. They were mostly useless as evidence since the scene had been cleaned up before the pictures were taken.

Despite that, looking at the dead woman, pale and shirtless, with her neck bent at a grisly angle, was unsettling. She barely looked human. Until now, Millicent Estrada had been an abstraction. But seeing her now, broken and vulnerable, Jessie felt a simultaneous surge of empathy and a burning desire to get justice for her.

She moved on to some online research on Estrada. It wasn't hard to find material. The sheer volume of photos alone was overwhelming. She and Beto were an extremely attractive couple but Millicent was especially stunning.

With long, dark hair that cascaded down in waves and facial features that seemed to have been sculpted by an artist, she had a fierceness that was almost too intense to be called beautiful. Her green eyes were especially compelling, as if they were calculating every person and scenario in real time. For some reason, she reminded Jessie of Arnold Schwarzenegger's cyborg character in *The Terminator*, who could do threat assessments of every humanoid he came in contact with in nanoseconds.

The pictures only scratched the surface. There were the straight news articles discussing the various cases she and husband Beto had handled, entertainment trade articles about the firm's work for their impressive celebrity client list, and finally the tabloid headlines about the couple's divorce and how they planned to keep the business running smoothly despite the split.

Everything sounded so amicable. But Jessie had long ago learned that things were rarely as rosy as they were presented in the press, especially by lawyers as media savvy as the Estradas. She decided that a visit to Mr. Estrada was in order. And she didn't want to wait until tomorrow. Showing up unexpectedly at his doorstep on a Sunday afternoon was more likely to generate an honest reaction than some massaged interview down at the station with his own lawyer in tow.

As soon as Hannah got back, she would call on Estrada to see if there were any unexpected thorns on those roses.

CHAPTER EIGHT

Jessie had a moment of doubt just before ringing Beto Estrada's doorbell.

After hearing Karen's tense phone exchange earlier about soccer parenting, she thought the woman might have other stuff on her mind and decided to do this interview solo. Normally, going to a potential suspect's home without a partner or backup would make her nervous. But in this case, she hoped that making the encounter casual might bear more fruit than something formal.

She wasn't going to trick an experienced attorney like Estrada into revealing information that put him in legal jeopardy. But maybe coming to his home by herself, not as a cop but a profiling consultant, would set him at ease enough to get him to lower his guard a bit.

And though she felt a little dirty about it, she suspected that interviewing him while he was potentially in the throes of grief after just losing his wife of seven years, even if they were no longer together, might work to her advantage. Besides, if he tried anything stupid, she had her gun and the self-defense training she'd received while attending the FBI Academy's ten-week program for local law enforcement.

Beto Estrada, who had moved out of the couple's house after the divorce, lived in a quaint rental cottage in the Miracle Mile section of Los Angeles, just a few blocks from Museum Row and the La Brea Tar Pits. The place wasn't much bigger than the guest house they'd found Cord Mahoney in this morning, but it was far more respectable, with a stone paver walkway, a Spanish-style, A-frame roof, and a lemon tree just off the porch.

She pushed any self-doubt out of her head as she rang the bell. Estrada opened the door within ten seconds. Just as in his pictures, he was a vaguely handsome man in his late forties, about a half-decade older than Millicent. He was tall and thin, with black hair and a conservative haircut that reminded Jessie of uniformed British schoolboys.

His eyes were red and puffy, though he appeared to have stopped crying a while ago. Unlike in his pictures, he wore glasses, and had on

41

blue jeans and a sweatshirt with "Rutgers" emblazoned on the front. It reminded her that both Estradas had fought hard to get where they were: New York City public schools, state universities, and finally Rutgers Law School, where they'd first met.

"Please tell me you're not with the press," he said. "I was hoping to get at least a few hours of peace."

"No, Mr. Estrada," she said, taking off her sunglasses and pulling out her ID. "I'm not with the press. But I'm afraid I can't offer you much in the way of peace. I'm Jessie Hunt. I'm a criminal profil—"

"I know who you are, Ms. Hunt. I didn't recognize you at first with the sunglasses. But in this city, you'd have to live under a rock to not be familiar with your reputation. And any lawyer who isn't probably doesn't deserve his degree."

Jessie wasn't entirely sure how to take that. Was it stopping multiple serial killers that made her memorable? Almost getting killed on numerous occasions? Or having her social media hacked and getting falsely accused of writing racist, vitriolic Facebook posts? She decided not to ask.

"Then you can guess why I'm here," she said, settling on cool professionalism as her default response.

"Milly?"

"Yes sir," she confirmed. "May I come in?"

"No detectives or uniformed officers with you?"

"I didn't think it would be necessary," she said confidently. "And since I've been tasked as the primary investigator, I wanted to get a jump on things while they're fresh."

"Of course, come in," Estrada said, opening the door for her and leading her to the small living room.

The television was paused. On the screen was a frozen image of Milly Estrada in a swimsuit on a beach, holding a glass of a red, tropical-looking concoction.

"What's that?" Jessie asked.

Estrada looked at the screen.

"That was from our anniversary vacation two years ago. We went to Maui."

He picked up the remote and pressed play. Milly Estrada came suddenly to life. She sipped from her straw and waved for him to stop filming.

"Are you trying to get me disbarred?" she asked playfully. "If footage of me half-drunk in a two-piece got out, I'd never score another high-profile client again."

"Are you kidding?" Beto Estrada asked from behind the camera. "If people saw how you look in that thing, it'd double your client list."

She smiled broadly as her face turned red.

"Turn that thing off and get over here," she purred.

A second later the clip ended. Jessie looked down at the floor briefly, feeling as if she'd just inappropriately spied on a deeply personal moment. But she quickly shook it off and looked up again, reminding herself that she was here to do a job and couldn't let sympathy get in the way. The man in front of her could be a murderer.

"I assume that this has been marked as an HSS case because of where Milly was killed?" he asked, quickly wiping away a tear as he turned off the TV.

"Why do you say that?" Jessie asked, taking a seat in a living room chair.

"Well, Milly was a brilliant litigator and represented many well-known clients. But I'm guessing that if she hadn't been found at Otis Estate, this would be handled by the regular division detectives."

Jessie saw no point in denying it.

"That's correct. The high profile of the man who owns the property certainly elevated it to HSS status."

He sat with that for a moment before responding.

"I guess if that's what it takes to get a real investigation going, it's worth it. I've heard that the police in that neck of the woods can be…malleable when it comes to aggressively pursuing their more powerful citizens."

"That perception seems to be pervasive," Jessie said, pulling out her notebook. "Do you mind if I ask you some questions?"

"You know, as unpleasant as that sounds, it's actually preferable to what I've been doing, which is sitting here, alternately going through old videos and photos and punching furniture. So fire away."

Jessie was slightly surprised at his willingness to engage but didn't waste any time lingering on it.

"Before we get to your ex-wife's death, I wanted to talk about you for a minute. Am I right to say that Mrs. Estrada handled most of the criminal work and your purview was more civil litigation?"

"That's right," Estrada said. "Our firm, Halsey, Burt, Tyler & Estrada, was previously just Halsey, Burt & Tyler. They handled a lot of contract work for tech companies, big banks, and corporate media. That's how Jasper Otis is affiliated with them. They represented him when he left All News Network and started News Channel America."

"When did you join up?" Jessie asked.

"We had our own firm in Secaucus, just across the river from the city. We represented some small media outlets, some second-tier personalities in film and TV. We handled a few deals for Halsey, Burt out there and they brought us in as associates about twelve years ago to help them expand into entertainment. We both made junior partner seven years ago and became named partners two years ago."

"So you two headed the entertainment division?" she confirmed.

"Yes," he said. "At first it was just us but as it expanded, each got our own teams. Last time I checked, Milly's unit was comprised of eleven attorneys and mine had fourteen. We were planning to hire an additional five in the new year."

"Okay, let's talk about her clients. Representing folks as narcissistic as actors, directors, and writers—things must have gotten volatile for her when cases didn't go her clients' way," she said, finally leading him down the difficult path leading up to her death.

He offered her a wry smile, fully aware of what she was doing.

"That's an understatement. There were some folks who acted as if *she* had committed the crime they'd been convicted of. But in the end, even her most irate clients had to admit that she served them well. Did you know that in over seventy criminal cases involving celebrity clients, sixteen of which involved felony charges, not a single one served a day in prison? Sure, a few had to spend some time in jail awaiting trial. But when it came down to it, she either got them off, got them probation, or got them time served. Some even got community service. Name another criminal lawyer for celebrities in this town who can say that. You can't."

"Did that make you jealous?" she asked.

He smiled once again.

"Do I sound jealous? I was proud of her."

"And yet you still got divorced."

Her comment seemed to make him drift off for a moment, as if consumed by a particularly vivid memory.

"Yes," he said, returning to the present. "It wasn't what I wanted. But after seventeen years together, seven of them married, Milly felt we'd drifted apart. There were no big fights or screaming matches. She

44

just told me one day over brunch that she loved me but wasn't *in* love with me anymore. She wanted more passion in her personal life."

"How did that make you feel?" Jessie asked, well aware that she sounded more like a therapist than an investigator.

"I was devastated. I was still in love with her, still am actually," he said, sounding wistful. "But I wasn't angry, just more wounded and disappointed. I guess that proved her point. If I was more outwardly upset, then maybe she would have never felt the need to end things. But I was more resigned to it than anything. So we worked it out, how we'd still make the firm work, the business side of things. It was surprisingly easy. Other than me moving out, the logistics weren't that complicated."

"It never ate at you?" Jessie asked skeptically.

"I can't say that," he conceded. "She'd come to work in more provocative dresses and wear a little more makeup than she used to. I didn't ask about it but I knew she was going to parties and having dates. That stung a little because she seemed to be having such a good time without me. But I also worried about her."

"Why?"

"She just really threw herself into the new lifestyle. I used to tease her about it, say that she was having the mid-life crisis instead of me. I know she did a lot more drinking and other chemicals, things she generally avoided prior to that. That's also when she started going to Jasper Otis's place a lot."

Jessie was hesitant to press the matter for fear that he'd shut down but knew she had no choice.

"Do you think they were involved?" Jessie asked, shifting uncomfortably.

He sighed as he weighed how to answer.

"I think she just enjoyed the perks of being in his orbit, though she did tell me he hit on her a few times. She said she wasn't interested, that she always found him to be a little creepy. I don't think he liked that. He's not used to being rejected."

"Is it possible that she was just denying it to avoid hurting you?"

He shrugged.

"I suppose. But she was pretty forthright with me about her other dalliances. I don't see why she'd hide that one."

Jessie decided she's warmed him up enough to go for it.

"Do you think Jasper Otis could have killed her?"

He didn't take long to respond.

45

"Yes."

"Why do you say that?" she asked.

"Like I said, he isn't used to being told no," Estrada said, sounding truly worked up for the first time. "That might have set him off. Otis presents a very cool, unruffled vibe, but I've seen him pissed off. It's not pretty. He has this coldness to him. Even if he wasn't upset, I could see him killing her just for the hell of it, to know what it feels like to snuff out the life of another human being. He's not wired like the rest of us, Ms. Hunt."

Jessie sat with that for a moment. Beto Estrada wasn't exactly an objective analyst, but he knew Otis better than her and his views couldn't be dismissed, even if they sounded outlandish.

"And where were you last night?" she asked, turning on a dime.

"Is this the part where I need to ask for my lawyer?" he wondered, now calm again.

"You certainly can," she said.

"That's okay," he replied, waving off the idea. "I was here. I did a little prep for a case I have this week, then watched a movie."

"On a streaming service?" she asked.

"That would have been helpful for an alibi, I suppose," he answered. "Easier to confirm, right? But no, I threw in an old DVD— *Sneakers* starring Robert Redford. You ever see it?"

"Can't say that I have," she said.

"Oh, you should check it out. It's a fun thriller."

"But unable to be verified," she noted.

"I suppose not. It's still in the machine, if you want to check. But I guess that doesn't help. I could have watched it a month ago and just left the DVD in there and you'd never know."

"You understand the problem," she said.

"Well, Ms. Hunt, I wish I could provide you with a more rock solid alibi to prove I didn't murder my ex-wife, but I didn't know I'd need one. Can't you just ask people who were there, show my picture around? There must be security footage. Surely my presence would be noted. As you know, we were a pretty high profile couple."

"Rest assured, we'll be doing all of that, Mr. Estrada," she said, standing up. "Something else I'd like to do is look through Millicent's work files. Are you able to help with that?"

He thought about it.

"I can't permit you to actually look in the files. That would be a breach of client confidentiality. But I don't see why you can't review her client list and what their cases were. Of course all of that is public record, but it would save you time to go straight to the source. If you think that would help with the investigation, I can expedite it."

"I'd appreciate it," she said.

"You should go today then," he told her as he walked her to the door. "It will be quieter on a Sunday, with fewer bureaucratic hoops to jump through. We have a weekend receptionist. I'll tell him to expect you. Security will have to remain with you at all times to ensure client privacy. But with those limitations, you'll have free access to whatever you think will help."

"Thank you," she said, hiding her surprise. Either Beto Estrada was sincere about wanting to find his ex-wife's killer or he really wanted to project that image.

She got in the car and was about to back out of the driveway. As she tried to think of the best route to the offices of Halsey, Burt, Tyler & Estrada, a sudden, terrifying thump on her window made her jump in her seat.

Beto Estrada was standing by the car. He looked winded and his eyes were wild. He had something in his hand, which he raised in her direction. She thought about going for her gun but knew she didn't have time. If he wanted to shoot her, he wasn't likely to miss.

CHAPTER NINE

Though she knew it was pointless, she dived forward, hoping the steering wheel might offer some protection from a potential bullet. She was preparing to put the car in reverse and punch the accelerator when a voice called out.

"It's not a gun."

She looked over. The object in Estrada's right hand, which he held out to her with a wildly flailing arm, was a thumb drive.

Jessie, ignoring the rush of adrenaline that made her extremities tingle, put the car in park and rolled down the window.

"You almost got shot," she said.

"I'm sorry," he said, breathing heavily. "I wanted to make sure to catch you."

"What is this?" she asked, a little short of breath herself.

"I wasn't going to tell you about this, but then I asked myself why I was holding onto it and I realized it was cowardice."

"You're not making sense, Mr. Estrada," she said, turning the car off.

His brow furrowed as if he was debating if he really wanted to go through with this. But he clearly knew, as she did, that it was too late to go back now.

"There's another reason I think Jasper Otis might be capable of killing someone," he said quietly. "I know what else he's capable of."

He pressed the thumb drive into her hand.

"What's on the drive?" she asked. A flutter of excitement rose in her chest.

"An interview."

"Care to expand on that?" she asked.

"I can't," he said, "other than to say it's extremely sensitive. I can't answer any questions about it. And I need you to swear that you won't reveal where you got it. If you say it was me, I'll deny it."

Jessie looked at Estrada, who seemed to almost be a different person from the man she'd talked to in the house. He was nervous, even a little scared.

"Why?" she asked.

"You'll understand when you hear it," he said. "Just be careful where you listen. And be careful who you share it with."

"Mr. Estrada, I can't make any promises—"

"Just listen," he insisted. "Then you'll understand."

He turned and walked quickly back into the cottage, never looking back. Jessie sat in the driveway, slightly stunned. After a few seconds, she turned the car back on and backed out, unsure what to do next. She had planned to go to the law firm but that suddenly seemed less pressing.

She considered going back to the station to play the interview there. But something about the intensity of Estrada's warning made her reluctant.

Great. I haven't even listened to the thing yet and it's making me paranoid.

Unable to wait any longer, she pulled into the parking garage of a nearby shopping plaza and followed the turns down to the lowest level. She parked, got out, and removed her laptop from her trunk. The garage radiated a heavy silence, muffling her footsteps. She looked around but didn't see a soul. On this level, there were only a couple of other vehicles, both unoccupied.

She got back in the car, locked the doors, turned on the laptop, and put in her headphones. She paused for a moment before inserting the thumb drive, wondering if it actually included a virus intended to delete her files.

Looking down at the hand holding the drive, she saw that it was trembling slightly. The anxiety of the moment threatened to overcome her. Estrada, despite his seeming openness, was still a source of suspicion. What if he was using her curiosity against her?

Shaking her head at how quickly she'd gone down the rabbit hole, she dismissed the theory and popped in the drive and clicked on the file.

Identified only by the name "Marla," it started to play. A male voice began to speak in what sounded like an empty room. His voice echoed off the walls.

"The date is April 19th, 2017. The time is 11:41 a.m. This is Detective Brian Shore commencing interview with subject Marla, not her real name. Are you ready to proceed?"

"Yes, sir," a female voice said meekly. She sounded about twelve.

"How old are you?"

"Fifteen."

"Where do you live?" Shore asked.

"I'm originally from Reseda but for the last few months I've been staying in Pacific Palisades."

"Can you describe your living situation?"

There was a brief silence, after which the detective added, "It's okay. You're safe now."

That seemed to give the girl the confidence to answer.

"It's a huge house. There are nine of us there, although the number of girls changes a lot. We share bedrooms, usually three but sometimes four per room."

"Are you there voluntarily?"

"We're kept there," she said. "They have security guards and a huge wall so that no one leaves without permission."

"What happens at the house?"

"That's where we're kept for when we're needed," she told him.

"Needed for what?"

"To have sex with the men," she said as if it was the most natural thing in the world.

Jessie gasped softly, then glanced around the garage to make sure no one had heard her despite the closed doors and windows. The detective continued.

"You were kept at this house against your will and men would come there to have sex with you, also against your will?"

"Yes," she confirmed. "I mean, I didn't fight it after the first few times. But I didn't want it."

"Did you recognize any of the men who came to the house?" Shore asked.

"No. But sometimes I was blindfolded. I think when that happened, I was with someone famous."

"Were you only made to have sex at this house?"

"No," she said. Jessie could tell from the quaver in the girl's voice that they were entering delicate territory.

"Where else?"

"I was taken on a private plane to a country where they spoke another language."

"Did you recognize the language?"

"Uh-uh," she said, sounding apologetic.

"That's okay," Detective Shore said. "Did you recognize anyone on the plane?"

There was no response.

"You can't just nod," Shore reminded her. "We need a verbal response."

"Yes, I recognized someone."

"Who was that?" he asked.

"The rich guy, Otis."

"Are you referring to Jasper Otis?"

"Uh-huh," she answered quietly.

"For the record, I am currently holding up a photograph of Jasper Otis. Is this the man from the plane?"

"Uh-huh."

"What happened on the plane?"

"On the plane?" she repeated. "Nothing. It didn't happen there. It was in the country."

"What happened when you got to the country?"

There was another brief pause. Jessie thought Detective Shore was going to have to cajole her again, but then she answered.

"Are you asking about what *he* did to me or what he let the other men do to me?"

Before he could reply, Jessie heard what sounded like a door opening. A second, extremely agitated male voice spoke.

"What the hell, Shore? I thought you were told to hand this case over."

"I just thought I'd get the ball rolling—" Shore started to say.

"This is an unauthorized interview with a minor, without parental consent. You could be suspended or worse. Shut off the tape."

"But sir—"

"Shut it off now!"

The tape ended and so did the audio file.

Jessie sat in her driver's seat for several seconds, stunned. Then she opened her door and started to retch. When she was done, she wiped her mouth and slammed the door shut. She needed to bring the drive to someone and there was only person she could trust.

CHAPTER TEN

She didn't knock before she burst through the door to Decker's office.

"Hunt!" he exclaimed, surprised and irritated. "You know I don't like people just barging in."

She closed the door and locked it, then glanced around the room, though she knew that was a waste of time.

"Do you have your office swept for bugs?" she asked. "Listening devices, I mean?"

His frown turned into a look of startled concern.

"Why?"

"Please, Captain," she insisted. "Just answer the question."

"Okay. Periodically, yes. Maybe twice a year."

"Are you able to get it done now?"

"I have to place a request." he said. "On a Sunday, it will take a few hours to get a team here. I have a portable scanner but it's not as sensitive as what the tech folks use."

"Are you able to come to my car? I need you to hear something."

Decker nodded immediately and followed her out to the police garage. Only when they were inside with the doors locked did she pull out the laptop.

"What is this about, Hunt?" he pressed.

"I'm about to play you an audio file," she told him. "But before I do, you need to know that I can't reveal how I got it. My source was adamant and I want to respect the person's wishes."

Decker looked like he was going to protest, but then seemed to think better of it.

"Play it," he said.

She did. Listening to it the second time around, she was able to pick up more clearly on the fear in Marla's voice and something very similar in Detective Shore's. She also noticed that he was moving the questioning along more quickly than in a standard interview, as if he knew he had limited time. It was clear now that it had taken place in an interrogation room. When it was over, Decker turned to her. His face was as white as a ghost. She'd never seen him so unsettled.

52

"Who else knows about this?" he asked.

"I have no idea. You're the only person I've shared it with. I don't know where my source got it, though I have some suspicions. It sounded to me like the supervisor who shut down the interview was anxious to keep it quiet. Do you know Detective Shore? Maybe he can shed some light on this."

"I'm afraid not," he said in a way that made her heart sink. "He's dead."

The anxiety that had been simmering in her gut started to boil.

"What happened?"

"Brian Shore died about four years ago, before you joined the force. He was in the Vice unit in West L.A. division. He was supposed to meet some buddies from his station for a fishing weekend at a cabin one of them has up near Big Bear. But his brakes gave out on the drive up the mountain. They found his car in a ravine about three hundred feet below the road. He was thrown out at some point. The coroner said the car rolled over him. They had to have a closed casket."

Jessie didn't respond. Her mind was racing. Was it possible that it was just a coincidence? Was there a reasonable explanation? Next to her Decker was tapping on the keyboard of his phone.

"You're not contacting anyone, are you?" she asked suddenly.

He looked at her as if she'd insulted his intelligence.

"I'm checking when exactly he died," he said as he scrolled. "It looks like it was April 21st, 2017. When was the interview again?"

"April 19th," Jessie said. "He died two days after this recording was made. He was killed over it, wasn't he?"

"We don't know that for sure," Decker said. "But it doesn't look good."

"And we have no idea who this girl Marla is," Jessie continued. "She could be dead too for all we know. How can we find out without revealing what we know?"

"Hunt, listen to me," he said, his voice cool. "The first thing we have to do is stay calm. Getting agitated doesn't do us any good."

"Excellent," she said, unable to rein in her sarcasm. "Staying calm here. Definitely *not* letting myself get freaked out that a billionaire media mogul may also be a pedophile involved in sex trafficking who possibly had a cop killed to keep it quiet, independent of being a suspect in a current murder investigation."

"Not the best effort I've ever seen on the calm front," Decker replied. "Don't jump the gun. Don't make assumptions. This looks bad

53

but we never actually heard Otis linked to a crime on that tape. It cut off before we got anything concrete. And we have no idea who this Marla is. It could all be a scam to blackmail Otis."

Jessie looked at him incredulously.

"Do you really believe any of that?" she asked.

"No. But I have to be open to the possibility that there's an innocent explanation for all this. Tunnel vision is our enemy, Hunt. See the whole field."

She couldn't contain her frustration.

"Okay, Coach. Then what's the next play?"

He let her tone slide.

"I'm taking this to Parker," he said.

Gaylene Parker ran Central Station's Vice unit. Jessie had worked with her on several occasions on cases that involved sex crimes. She had always seemed like a competent straight shooter, but this wasn't any old case.

"Are you sure—?" she began.

"I trust her implicitly," he said before she finished the thought. "I've known her for a decade and she's the best there is. I'll go only to her to keep the circle tight, no other detectives from the unit."

"That's fine," Jessie said. "But I can't tell her where the audio came from either. Now I know why my source was so worried. They must have found out what happened to Shore."

"I'll be very discreet," Decker assured her. "I won't even say it came from you if you don't want."

Jessie thought he was being eminently reasonable, so she decided to try one more long shot.

"Maybe we just bring Otis in on the pretext of talking about the Estrada case, then mention this in passing to see how he reacts."

He looked at her like he shouldn't even have to dignify that.

"Come on, Hunt," he said. "You know better than that. Bringing him in now would be the worst possible move. We have nothing on him for this. We don't even have a victim. And unless you're holding out on me, you don't have anything on him yet in the Estrada murder either. We're probably only going to get one shot at this guy before his phalanx of lawyers closes ranks. We need to have all our ducks in a row when we make our move. We have to be methodical—no mistakes."

Jessie knew he was right. But she couldn't stop the connections from forming in her mind, even if there was no proof to bear them out.

54

"What if the cases are connected, Captain? What if Millicent Estrada was killed because she knew about this? Maybe the broken neck and missing top are just designed to throw us off and make us think there's a sex component."

Decker closed her laptop for her and put the thumb drive in his pocket, a sign that he considered this conversation over.

"Maybe all that's true, Hunt. But spinning theories doesn't do us much good. You have to prove it. So go out there and do your job. Find Millicent Estrada's killer. Let me worry about the recording. If they end up connecting, we'll deal with that too. But right now, your job is to solve this murder. Got it?"

She nodded reluctantly.

"Where are you headed now?" he asked.

"To her law firm to see if any cases she handled suggest motive."

"Good," he said, getting out of the car. "Take Detective Bray with you. You need someone to help keep you grounded right now."

"Yes, Captain."

He started to close the door, then stopped himself.

"And Hunt, don't mention any of this to her. Until we know more, this is strictly 'need to know' and she doesn't."

At least they agreed on that.

CHAPTER ELEVEN

Karen Bray was already waiting when Jessie got there.

The offices of Halsey, Burt, Tyler & Estrada were located in a massive tower in Century City, just a long red carpet's walk away from the building that served as Nakatomi Plaza in *Die Hard*. This skyscraper wasn't as celebrated but it was equally impressive, forty stories high and housing at least a dozen of the most prominent firms in the city.

"You ready for this?" Jessie asked when she met Karen at the main entrance to the office on the thirty-seventh floor.

"It was this or noshing on chips and bean dip while watching three-hundred-pound men wearing pads slam into each other for a few hours. I think I made the right choice."

"How did the soccer game go?" Jessie asked, not wanting to directly probe her new partner about the state of her marriage.

Karen smiled, obviously not fooled.

"I didn't know you were such a fan, Jessie," she said, before adding, "The Hornets—that's Ryan's team—won five to three. They celebrated with pizza and ice cream and then more pizza."

"Your son's name is Ryan?"

Karen nodded.

"I didn't want to say anything, for obvious reasons."

"I appreciate that, but it's okay," Jessie told her. "It's not like I don't think about my Ryan five hundred times a day anyway. You mentioning your son isn't going to send me on a misery bender, at least not one worse than I'm already on."

"Then you're made of stronger stuff than me," Karen said. "If anything like that happened to my husband, Cal, my already brittle hair would be completely gone."

Jessie nodded, not saying anything about the conversation she overheard. Karen smiled again.

"Surprised to hear that? Don't be. We have our moments, my hubby and I, but he's a good guy and a good man. He just tends to forget that when his team is playing, so I remind him."

"Not my business," Jessie said.

"You'll get there too one day," Karen said.

Jessie couldn't help but laugh.

"I don't know about that. The last guy I married is the main reason that my life's in the toilet right now."

"Yeah, but your Ryan's not like that, right? It'll be different this time."

Something about the comment threw Jessie. The idea that she might one day marry Ryan Hernandez wasn't new to her. But ever since his injury, she'd put thoughts like that on the back burner. The fact that someone else seemed to think it ought not to be made her wonder why she wasn't so sure.

"So Estrada just volunteered to let us come here?" Karen asked, snapping her out of her personal crises.

"No, I asked him. But I think he was anxious to do anything that would prove he was helping."

She proceeded to fill the detective in on the particulars of the interview.

"Do you like him for this?" Karen asked when she finished.

"He has no real alibi and the ex should always be near the top of the suspect list, as I can attest to. But he was pretty straightforward with me and seemed to genuinely want this solved. If he's lying, he's very good at it. Plus, it's clear that he still loved her. The question is whether that got twisted somehow."

"Your people are doing facial recognition from the party, right?" Karen asked. "To see if he showed up?"

"Absolutely," Jessie assured her. "I don't trust his phone GPS. He could have left it at the house. That's why I called our top researcher, Jamil Winslow, on the way here. He's going to do a deep dive on Estrada's tech tomorrow. Maybe the guy ordered food last night. Maybe he was posting online. Maybe a security camera caught him leaving the house. Anything he finds will be more than we have now."

"You don't want Ernie Purcell to honcho that stuff?" Karen asked jokingly.

"I think that the less we involve Purcell in this case," Jessie replied, "the more likely we are to solve it. And I get the sense he's happy to step aside so he can avoid getting squeezed from all sides."

Before Karen could respond, the door opened.

"I'm sorry," said a young man in a sweater vest and jeans. "I saw you on the security camera. Is one of you Jessie Hunt?"

Jessie raised her hand.

"I am. And this is Detective Bray."

"Wonderful," he said. "My name is Simon. Mr. Estrada let me know you'd be coming by and asked me to make Ms. Estrada's client and case lists with synopses available for your review. I've set everything up in the large conference room."

He led them down the hall in silence for several seconds, then looked back.

"I was so sorry to hear about Ms. Estrada," he said.

"Did you know her well?" Karen asked.

"No. Only passing in the halls," he admitted. "But I hoped to make her team one day. She was a real trailblazer. Did you know that no entertainment industry client of hers ever served a single day in prison?"

"I think I heard that somewhere," Jessie said.

They reached the conference room, which was indeed large. The table alone had to be a good forty feet long. A burly man in a navy suit stood at the far end of the room.

"That's Ajax," Simon said. "He's here to…ensure everything runs smoothly for you."

"That's okay, Simon," Karen said. "We know why he's here. You can dispense with the euphemisms."

"Yes, ma'am," Simon said, his face turning red. "There's water in the mini-fridge behind the cabinet on the back wall. If you need anything else, just have Ajax buzz me and I'll bring it in."

After he left, Jessie and Karen moved over to the pile of paper in the middle of the conference table. Ajax joined them, standing just off to the side. Up close, Jessie saw that he was even more massive than she originally thought. Easily six foot six and two hundred fifty pounds, he looked like he might have just come from playing in the football game Karen's husband had been watching. His head was shaved and his hands, the size of oven mitts, had red, angry scars on the knuckles.

"Good afternoon, ladies," he said. "I'm sure this will just be a formality, but I need to go over the ground rules with you. First, what you have on the table is a list of Ms. Estrada's clients who have had cases they've had before the court, along with abstracts describing the cases. If you need actual court documents, Simon can try to provide those, as long as they were in the public record. All other materials are off-limits, I'm afraid."

"What about clients who didn't have any cases?" Jessie asked. "Maybe folks who just kept her on retainer?"

Ajax shook his head.

"Unless specifically authorized, that material is unavailable. We're providing data on people who Ms. Estrada represented in matters before the court. If you have a particular request beyond that, you'll need to make it formally."

Though Jessie didn't like having the parameters of her search limited, she wasn't in a position to be too demanding. After all, without a warrant, the firm was under no obligation to allow the access she currently had. She decided not to rock the boat for now.

"Okay," she said, turning to Karen. "I think we should be looking specifically for two things. Tell me if you disagree."

"Shoot."

"First, were any of Estrada's clients investigated for crimes resembling what happened to her—violence towards women, assault, that kind of thing?"

"Makes sense," Karen agreed.

"Second, were any of her clients unhappy with the outcome of their case? That information won't necessarily be in the files. We'll have to cross-reference with news reports to check on that."

"Bonus for you," Karen pointed out, "as a detective who has had an unusual number of law enforcement interactions with celebrities, I may remember some of them."

"You've got that over me. As you may have learned from the last case we worked on, I'm not exactly a pop culture expert."

"I've got you covered," Karen said. "I didn't want to say it earlier because it sounds like they made your life hell, but I'm a regular reader of Blabber."

"I won't hold it against you," Jessie promised.

They split up the cases alphabetically and dived in. The first thing Jessie checked was to see if Jasper Otis had been honest about Milly Estrada not personally representing him. At least based on the documents that she had available, he had been. Then she started to go through everything again, looking for the name "Marla," on the off chance she was mentioned, but it was a needle in a haystack.

"Do you have a digitized version of this stuff?" she asked Ajax.

"Not one that we can share," he answered. "Separating out the confidential data from the public facing material is much harder on the computer. That's why we gave you hard copies instead."

Jessie looked at her watch. She'd already spent fifteen minutes on this wild goose chase. She reminded herself of what Decker had said. He would follow up on the Marla interview with Detective Parker. In the meantime, she needed to stay focused on the case in front of her, on solving Milly Estrada's murder.

She began working her way methodically through the files. It quickly became clear that, while none of Milly's clients actually served prison time, a number of them were held in jail for long stretches before and during trials. One guy—a well-known rock star named Percy Avalon—was held in custody for nine months on charges that he held a model from one of his music videos against her will in a hotel bathroom.

When the case finally came to trial, a member of his entourage claimed that he had confined the woman without Percy's knowledge. That guy was sentenced to fourteen months in prison. Percy, who was convicted of an accessory charge, got time served. Jessie marked him down as someone she'd like to chat with, especially if she could confirm he was at the party.

In another instance, an actor named Rance Jensen got himself in some real trouble. The former star of a TV series called *Batts' Badge* about a hard-driving sheriff in a corrupt small town, Jensen was charged with assault after he beat up a reporter who asked him about allegations that he was verbally abusive on the set.

Interestingly, Milly Estrada handed off his case to another firm just before trial, claiming an unspecified conflict of interest. Jensen was convicted and spent four months in prison. His comments after his release suggested he thought Estrada had bailed on him rather than risk ruining her perfect "no prison" record. He sounded particularly salty about it. Jessie wrote him down as a person to look at more. She noticed that his wasn't an isolated incident.

"Hey," she said to Karen, "are you finding that Estrada dumped a lot of cases that looked like losers just before trial?"

"Now that you mention, I have seen a few," Karen said. "At least three that I can remember."

"Let's keep tabs on those folks," Jessie said. "I suspect that if she ran into anyone at the party who she jettisoned before trial, their conversations might not have been too friendly."

*

60

They'd gone through the files and collected a list of eight people who either had a history of violence, were left by Estrada at the trial altar, or both. Jessie called Jamil Winslow's work line to leave a message asking him to focus on them when he started poring over the footage from Otis Estate tomorrow.

She already had him going through Beto Estrada's alibi, and under normal circumstances, adding this to his punch list might have been asking too much. But ever since she'd first worked with him on a murder case in the wealthy beach community of Manhattan Beach, he'd proven to be a savant.

Short and skinny, at twenty-four, Jamil was brilliant, persistent, and seemingly immune to exhaustion. He'd actually left the Manhattan Beach PD to join her station, specifically to work with her and Ryan, a source of guilt for her considering that she now only intermittently consulted for the force.

To her surprise, he picked up.

"What are you doing there, Jamil?" she demanded. "It's Sunday afternoon."

"I wanted to get a jump on the Beto Estrada stuff and I figured it would be easier from the office," he said as if it was the most natural thing in the world.

"Don't you have things to do?" she asked.

"This is a thing to do," he insisted. "What's up?"

She explained what she wanted. When she was done, the unexpected silence on the other end of the line immediately told her there was an issue.

"What's wrong?" she asked.

"I was going to wait until tomorrow to tell you this," he finally replied. "But the folks in tech have some bad news. There's a problem with the security footage from Otis Estate. There are gaps."

"What does that mean?"

"According to the security chief at the estate, with the exception of the main entrance to South House, they don't save the recordings unless there is something notable. There are six security officers in a dedicated facility on the estate monitoring the footage in real time. If there's nothing suspicious, they delete the files every hour. As a result, there are huge sections of time in multiple areas on the estate that have no coverage."

Jessie tried to keep her voice even, not wanting to take her frustration out on him.

"Do you buy that?" she asked.

She could almost hear him shrug.

"It's not inconceivable," he admitted. "With the sheer volume of raw footage that place accumulates, it would become unwieldy pretty fast. But you'd think they'd want to hold onto the stuff a little longer after a party, if only for liability issues. As it turns out, the material we do have is mostly still there because of money."

"Money?" she repeated.

"Yeah, Tech says the best stuff we have is from the camera across from the entrance to the main house. Apparently they kept that active and recording all the time to tally the total number of attendees in order to better track catering needs."

"So the only workable footage we have exists because they want to make sure they had enough food?" Jessie confirmed.

Before Jamil could reply, her phone alarm went off. It was the reminder to give Ryan his meds.

"I have to go," she said. "We'll talk tomorrow."

After hanging up, she noticed a text from earlier she must have missed. It was from Nurse Patty: *Leaving for the day. Reviewed Ryan's status with Hannah. See you tomorrow.*

A wave of shame washed over her. She'd been so immersed in the research that she'd been gone all afternoon and never thought about it. She'd insisted that this case wouldn't interfere with her personal life and yet she was getting sucked in again.

And there was more. Despite the relaxed nature of the text, a burst of apprehension shot through Jessie. The idea of leaving Ryan alone in her sister's care made her uneasy.

"Excuse me," she said to Karen as she dashed from the room. "I have to make a call."

CHAPTER TWELVE

"So you don't trust me."

Hannah couldn't decide if she felt more offended or put upon.

"I didn't say that," Jessie told her. "If I didn't trust you, I wouldn't have let Nurse Patty leave. I just wanted to review the medications with you since it's the first time you're giving them to him."

"You didn't *let* Patty leave," Hannah reminded her. "She was going no matter what and now you're trying to make it sound like it was all part of your grand plan to entrust me with responsibility. But I already told you that Patty walked me through the meds, so this feels a lot like you're checking up on me."

She could feel the resentment building in her.

"I didn't mean it that way," Jessie insisted. "I'd be hypervigilant no matter who was giving him the meds, myself included. It just happens to be you doing it right now."

Hannah knew that she should have some sympathy for her sister's situation, and yet she couldn't help going in for the kill. Jessie had been taking her for granted all day and she deserved to be put in her place.

"And why is it that I'm doing it right now?' she asked rhetorically before answering her own question. "Could it be because on the very day that your invalid boyfriend is released to your care from the hospital, you're running around the city on a Sunday afternoon, chasing down a case that can't possibly be as important as what's going on here?"

The silence on the other end of the line told her that she'd hit pay dirt with that. She felt a satisfaction only slightly moderated by the sense that maybe she'd gone too far. She continued before her sister could try to reprimand her.

"I'll give him his meds. I'll feed him his gruel. But maybe you can try to get back here in time to put him to bed, if that's not too much to ask."

She hung up without waiting for a reply, then sat on the couch, seething silently. The truth was, she'd already given Ryan his meds even before Jessie had called her. She'd also helped him reposition himself on the bed and turned on a fan because he had grunted "hot" to

63

her. When he'd asked about his girlfriend's whereabouts with the word "Jessie," Hannah had soothingly assured him that she'd be back soon, not having any idea if it was true.

Now she was stuck here in this house, on a sunny Sunday afternoon, while a barely functional human wheezed in a bedroom down the hall. It wasn't fair. She tried the deep breathing technique Dr. Lemmon had taught her in a recent therapy session, one the woman claimed was especially effective at what she called "releasing the steam." It wasn't working.

So she decided to call Kat. Katherine "Kat" Gentry was Jessie's best friend. Of late, she'd also proven to be a good sounding board. Hannah had only recently started at a new high school and, considering it was her senior year and she didn't know anyone, she didn't have much in the way of confidantes.

But Kat was different. In addition to being a badass former Army Ranger with the scars to prove it, the woman had also run security at a penal facility holding mentally unstable killers. When that went awry, she'd become a private investigator. In other words, she wasn't one to mess with.

More importantly, she could keep a secret. It was only a few weeks ago that Kat had taken her on a stakeout of a drug dealer, during which Hannah had confronted the guy for no reason other than to feel the rush of danger—to feel anything really.

Later that night, when Kat had threatened to tell Jessie what happened, Hannah confessed the truth: that she only seemed capable of feeling emotions when she put herself in extreme situations, and that she worried Jessie would abandon her if she found out just how damaged she was.

It had been a relief to tell Kat the truth, something she hadn't been able to tell Jessie or even Dr. Lemmon. Kat had promised not to reveal what she'd been told, as long as Hannah promised not to put herself at risk like that again.

And in the intervening weeks, they'd both followed through. Hannah had restrained her urge to push beyond safe boundaries. And Kat had listened patiently as she tried to work out the conflicts in her head. She knew that at some point, Kat would insist that she come clean with the people responsible for her, but she hadn't done so yet and Hannah was grateful.

"What's up, Hanna Barbera?" Kat asked upon picking up, using a nickname that Hannah didn't understand.

"Nothing much," Hannah replied. "What's up with you?"

"Just driving back from a weekend at my honey's."

Kat was long-distance dating a sheriff's deputy from Lake Arrowhead, a small town in the mountains about eighty miles northeast of L.A. She sounded happy. Hannah was reluctant to ruin her mood with her own problems.

"Ryan arrives today, right?" Kat said.

"He's actually already here, has been for a few hours now."

"How that going?"

"Okay. Jessie had to leave for a case and the nurse left a little while ago too. So it's just the two of us."

"Oh," Kat said, and Hannah could almost hear the woman processing the situation. "That must be fun for you."

"I've had better afternoons," she admitted.

"Well, I know Jessie really appreciates what you're doing. She told me how excited she was to have Ryan coming to stay at the house. So if she's not there, this case must be serious."

"They're *all* serious, Kat," Hannah said bitterly.

"It's just one day, right?" Kat said, skipping over her tone. "Tomorrow you'll be back in school and there will be a nurse available to help."

"Yeah, during the day," Hannah countered irritably. "What happens at night when she's working on a lead and I'm the only one here?"

She could sense Kat struggling for an acceptable answer. She let her squirm.

"Listen," Kat finally said. "Your sister has got some resources available. If she has to invest in a night nurse too, she will. Frankly, I think that's a good idea regardless, especially for the first few weeks. Maybe I can broach the idea with her. In the meantime, I should be back in the city in about an hour and a half. Do you want me to stop by?"

Hannah did but knew it was asking too much.

"That's okay," she said. "Ryan's sleeping and I'm sure Jessie will be back by then. I'll get by."

"You sure?"

"Yeah, I'm fine."

"Hey, Hanna Barbera, do me a favor," Kat said, upbeat.

"What?"

"Walk into the bathroom and look in the mirror."

"What for?"

"Just do it," she instructed.

Hannah complied, turning on the light and staring at herself.

"What do you see?" Kat asked.

"Myself."

"Come on, you can do better than that."

"I see a girl," Hannah said, "with sandy blonde hair that probably needs to be cut, green eyes that have too much red in them, someone tall enough to borrow my sister's clothes when she doesn't know I'm doing it, cute enough to get a boyfriend until he realizes what a dumpster fire I am. How's that?"

"So if I can rephrase, you're a tall, blonde-haired, green-eyed hottie who has good fashion sense and isn't too full of herself. Fair?"

Hannah couldn't help but laugh.

"Remind me to have you rework my online dating profile," she said.

"Please tell me you don't have one of those."

"I'm just messing with you," Hannah allowed.

"Thank god. An inability to feel standard human emotions I can handle. Dating, not so much. You get my point though, right?"

"What's your point?" Hannah asked.

"You've got a lot going for you. You're healthy. You're smart. You've got a roof over your head. You've got a sister who loves you. And you've got me. Try to look at the positives."

Hannah smiled despite herself. Kat was trying so hard. She decided to throw her a bone.

"You know, you're really turning me around here. I think I may apply to Harvard on one of those runway model scholarships."

The comment made her flash back to an odd conversation she'd had at school a few weeks ago with a girl who had also suggested that her good looks might work to her financial advantage.

"I got one of those," Kat said, bringing Hannah back to the present. "But I joined the army instead."

Hannah could tell the time for serious discussion had ended.

"I'm going to let you go. I've taken up enough of your time bitching about my life. Bask in your romance."

"You're sure you're good?" Kat asked.

"Good enough."

After she hung up, Hannah decided to go lie in the hammock in the back yard. Before that, she slipped into Ryan's room to open his window so she could hear if he called out for help. He was fast asleep.

66

For half a second, she imagined herself pulling the pillow out from underneath his head and pressing it against his face, smothering him, and releasing him from the pain of his current existence.

The moment passed and she went outside. As she settled into the hammock, she allowed herself to buy into the image of herself that Kat had described. A picture of her sashaying down a fashion runway, wearing a cap and gown, filled her drowsy thoughts.

For now at least, as she drifted off, the idea of mercy killing her sister's boyfriend faded away. When she eventually woke up, it was to the sound of Ryan moaning in pain.

CHAPTER THIRTEEN

Jessie thought he'd have a nicer house.

As she and Karen arrived at the home of Rance Jensen in their separate cars, she noted that the place was officially impressive. It was a two-story, Spanish mission–style home with elaborate designs on the exterior wall tile. But on closer inspection, the shingles were in disrepair. The grass in the yard was getting shaggy, and the paint job looked worn. For a big TV star, the guy didn't seem to be keeping up appearances.

Before they went to the door, they went over their plan. This was the only guy on the list of suspects they'd developed at the law firm who they knew for certain had been at the party last night. At least two revelers they'd interviewed by the pool mentioned his name, specifically referring to his body autographing skills, so he seemed like a good choice to start with until Jamil got to look at the security footage.

"Be ready," Jessie advised. "We already know the guy's volatile. Whether he did this or not, we've seen that he's capable of violence. That reporter he beat up still can't see out of one eye and it's been three years."

"Got it," Karen said in a tone that suggested she didn't need any extra warnings. "Bad man likes to hit. Prepare to hurt."

Jessie reminded herself that she was dealing with a pro and that her words of caution were not only unnecessary but a little insulting.

"Sorry," she said.

Karen winked and with the mini-dispute resolved, they walked up to the front door, where the detective rang the bell. She had to press it twice more before the door was opened by a skinny, thirty-something guy in a bathrobe. His blond hair was in full bed head mode and he yawned for a good five seconds before speaking.

"I don't do autographs at my home," he said irritably, squinting at them through puffy hazel eyes.

"We're not here for autographs, Mr. Jensen," Karen said. "We're—"

"I don't give freebies either," he said. "If I had a dime for every professional mom who wanted to have a poke with Sheriff Batts, I'd probably have herpes."

The two women looked at each other, sharing a moment of annoyance.

"That's not why we're here either—" Jessie started to say before he cut her off too.

"Now you, I might take the risk and do," he said, looking her up and down.

Jessie wasn't sure whether to be more pissed at his aggressive ogling or his crass dismissal of Karen. Ultimately she decided not to indulge her anger about either.

"As flattering as that is, sir," she said, "we're with the police and we need you to answer a few questions."

Jensen laughed.

"That's a new one," he said. "I kind of like it. Were you planning to read me my rights and then cuff me? Maybe you're anticipating a rough interrogation, one that might get physical?"

Jessie could sense that Karen wanted to take this one and deferred to her.

"Detective Karen Bray," she said, holding up her badge and ID with one hand as she casually pulled back her jacket to reveal the sidearm attached to her belt. "This is Jessie Hunt. She's a criminal profiler. As she said, we have some questions for you. You can answer them here at your home, in your bathrobe. Or we can make this more formal down at the station. It's your call, Mr. Jensen."

He looked at Karen's ID, then back at her unamused face before turning back to Jessie, who was equally taciturn.

"This is real?" he asked. "You're not messing with me?"

"We're not messing with you," Jessie said, deciding to launch in before he got his wits about him. "We understand that you were at a party at the Otis Estate last night, is that correct?"

"What of it?" he demanded, recovering faster than she anticipated.

"What do you think of Jasper Otis?" she asked.

Jensen shrugged.

"Rich dude, generous. Keeps quality liquor and hot, young girls around. What's not to like?"

"Ever see him lose his cool? Get angry?"

"I don't know him that well," Jensen said. "Why?"

"Did you run into any old acquaintances while you were there?" Karen wondered, jumping in quickly.

Jessie picked up on what the detective was hoping to do and liked the idea. By alternately peppering Jensen with questions, batting him back and forth like a tennis ball, she hoped to keep him off balance long enough to get something worthwhile out of him. It was worth a shot.

"It was a huge party. I knew lots of people there," he said.

"What do you think of Millicent Estrada?" Jessie asked.

He stared at her curiously before answering.

"She's a bitch."

"Why do you say that?" Karen asked.

"Because she left me hanging just before I went to court on a bogus assault charge. She was supposed to be this superstar lawyer but when she got worried that she couldn't win, she cut me loose. I ended up serving a hundred twenty-two days in prison, where I had to have three guards escort me from my solitary holding cell to the yard for workouts, all because there was a risk that another inmate might want to make me his personal trophy. So yeah, not a fan. Why?"

"She's dead, Mr. Jensen," Jessie said, watching him closely as she spoke. "And she was at the party last night. So we're wondering if you ran into her at any point?"

His eyes went wide for a moment, though Jessie couldn't tell whether it was shock at the news or fear at the unspoken accusation. Impressively, it only lasted a second before he regained his disdainful, gruff manner.

"I think you should talk to my lawyer. I had to get a new one, you know."

"Are you sure that's how you want to handle it, Mr. Jensen?" Karen asked, as if she was concerned for him. "We ask a simple question about your whereabouts and you immediately refer us to your lawyer?"

"What were you expecting?"

"I don't know," Karen said, "maybe a word of compassion about her loss? A question about how it happened? A firm denial that you saw her at any point? An offer to provide a list of people who were with you and could verify that you didn't interact with her? Any of those, I could understand. But 'talk to my lawyer'?" That tends to make us law enforcement types perk up."

He looked at her imperviously.

"Hey, anything that makes you a little perkier is a plus, I'd say. You're looking pretty run down, Detective."

"Is that really the response you want to stick with?" Jessie asked, jumping in before Karen got the urge to reply in kind. "I mean, we obviously know you were there. We've already spoken to people who attended about your...proclivities. We're pulling footage from the dozens of cameras on the property that will verify how you spent your time. And yet, you seem intent on alienating the very people who will determine how aggressively to pursue you as a person of interest. That seems like a dicey way to go. You want to take one more shot at it? Amid all the activities you partook in last night, did you see Millicent Estrada at any point?"

She knew she was taking a risk. No one they'd spoken to had specifically mentioned Jensen doing anything illegal and she doubted they'd get any incriminating footage. But unless he was confident that he'd been a good boy, she figured she could instill a little doubt in him.

Rance Jensen looked at each of them separately, then, very casually, undid the belt of his robe so that it fell open, revealing that he was wasn't wearing anything underneath.

"I'm in my home," he said slowly. "This is harassment. Talk to my lawyer."

He slammed the door shut. Jessie and Karen shared stunned looks.

"I'd say we should arrest him for public indecency," Karen said, half-chuckling. "But I think there needs to be more visual evidence than he provided to justify the charge."

Jessie shrugged, trying to hold back her own laughter.

"At least we know he's not armed," she said.

That broke open the dam. As they walked back to their cars, they erupted into a fit of giggling. When they finally recovered, Karen spoke.

"As much as I'd like to take him in for general assholery, I think we're stuck for now. Maybe we'll get lucky with some footage, but he seems to know we're hamstrung."

"Let's not give up just yet. If anyone can find something, it's Jamil," Jessie said as her phone rang. "Maybe that's him now."

She looked at the screen. It was Hannah.

"What's up?" she asked when she picked up.

"You have to get back here now," her sister said breathlessly. "Ryan fell."

CHAPTER FOURTEEN

"I'm fine," Ryan said for the third time.

It was no more convincing than the first two.

He didn't look hurt. And he was alert and responsive. Despite that, Jessie could see that Hannah was extremely upset. Jessie told her to wait for her outside as she settled Ryan back into bed.

She could feel a vise of guilt and worry wrapping around her and fought it off, knowing that she couldn't show weakness in front of him. He needed her strong right now. She'd deal with her own culpability later.

"What were you thinking?" she demanded, trying to keep the frustration out of her voice.

"Rehab," he said after much effort.

Jessie made sure her voice was composed when she replied.

"We have someone coming in for that tomorrow, Ryan," she insisted. "I know you want to get back to normal as soon as you can. But it's your first day here. You were in the hospital this morning. Be at least a little patient, please."

He nodded, though she could tell he wasn't convinced.

"What?" she asked. "I can tell you're holding back."

He stared at her. His eyes were blazing but his lips were pursed with the effort of trying to speak.

"Burden," he finally managed to blurt out.

She sighed and sat down next to him on the bed.

"You're not a burden," she insisted. "I love you. What did you think—that your girlfriend was just going to take a hard pass on caring for you while you get better? That's insulting. Besides, the department is paying for your medical and rehab bills, so that's not an issue. I want you here. So does Hannah. And this house is perfect for your recovery. It's like it was meant to be."

He shook his head, unconvinced. She tried again.

"I know you're frustrated, babe. You like to charge hard, all the time. But you have to cut yourself some slack. Did you think you were going to be back on the streets this week, chasing down criminals? It's going to be slower than you like. But we'll get there if you don't delay the process by getting injured while pushing too hard, too fast."

She looked at him, hoping she could will him to feel her love and support. He opened his mouth and, after a few seconds of struggle, managed to get out another word.

"Useless," he said, his voice choked with frustration.

Her shoulders slumped involuntarily.

"Okay," she said gently. "I'm going to go prep some soup and a smoothie for your dinner. I think the late football game started a little while ago so I'll put that on for you. I'll be back in a few minutes."

She left the room with a smile plastered on her face, fully aware that he was watching for any sign that she had given up on him. Hannah was sitting at the kitchen island.

"How is he?" she asked.

"Agitated, discouraged, irate, take your pick. How are you?"

Hannah looked at her without any of her usual cynicism.

"I was really scared. I was outside resting in the hammock and I heard this thud. When I got inside, he was on the floor. I knew he hadn't just fallen out of the bed because the sidebar was up. It was like he tried to walk somewhere, but he didn't even use the walker. At first he wouldn't even let me help him up."

She looked away quickly.

Jessie thought she might be fighting back tears and it broke the dam inside her, one she hadn't realized was holding so much back. This was her fault. She should have been here to prevent this, to protect her already traumatized sister from carrying another burden that wasn't hers.

"I'm really sorry," she said. "I had no idea he'd try something like that. Clearly I misjudged his desire to get moving, even at the expense of good sense. I shouldn't have left you here to take care of him alone, even for a short time."

It looked like Hannah was about to agree with her, but the girl seemed to catch herself. When she spoke her voice was firm.

"I really think we should have an in-house nurse all the time for the first few weeks—day and night. With me at school and you taking this case, it's just too much. What if I'm in the bathroom when he tries this again? We need to have the ability to get groceries or take a walk and know he's safe."

Jessie nodded.

73

"You're right," she said. "In fact, Kat texted something similar to me earlier. I guess I thought—more like hoped—that we could handle the nights. But that was clearly overly optimistic, at least for now. After I get him squared away for the evening, I'll call the service. This will be the only night we have to honcho this alone. I promise. He won't love it but he'll just have to deal."

She paused for a moment before changing subjects.

How was your day?"

Hannah gave her a "you're kidding, right?" look.

"Maybe we should just talk about *your* day," she suggested. "Interesting case?"

Jessie decided to forgo her usual closemouthed attitude toward cases in the interest of changing subjects.

"It's certainly high profile," she answered as she got out the smoothie fixings. "A woman was murdered at the Otis Estate."

"Otis Estate as in Jasper Otis, the rich jerk?"

"The very same," Jessie confirmed.

"Is he a suspect?" Hannah asked, animated in a way she hadn't been moments earlier.

"You know I can't get into that. But I promise that once we solve the case, I'll share all the juicy details."

"Can you at least tell me who the victim is?"

"No one famous," Jessie said. "It's just a normal woman. But what was done to her was pretty awful. The bastard who did it is going to rot if I have anything to say about it."

Her thoughts drifted to the anonymous "Marla." She wondered if she'd ever get to be so definitive about the punishment for *her* abusers.

"What aren't you telling me?" Hannah asked.

Jessie continued to be amazed at how perceptive Hannah was at picking up on nonverbal cues and how often she still underestimated her own sister.

"I was actually thinking about something else," she said as she tossed protein powder and fruit into the blender. "I stumbled across another potential case while working this one, involving potential sex trafficking of teenage girls, right here under our noses. They supposedly even house a bunch of them at a fancy mansion. I'm just wondering how much of that sort of thing sneaks below the radar, maybe in schools like yours, because these girls have been indoctrinated into a culture of silence, made to feel like this is what they deserve."

Hannah seemed to be seriously pondering the question.

"Have you ever thought of putting undercover cops in the schools where you think it's happening? Maybe you need someone with street level perspective to see what you can't."

Jessie considered the idea. It wasn't a bad one.

"That could work," she said. "But we have so little information. It would hard to know where to start."

She hit the blender and they both watched the blueberries, strawberries, and bananas turn into a purple mush. When Jessie shut it off, Hannah spoke up.

"Well, I'll keep my eyes open at school tomorrow. If I see any sketchy-looking older dudes on campus handing out business cards, looking for sex slaves, I'll let you know."

"Thanks," Jessie said, smiling bitterly. "That's probably as effective as anything I could do right now."

*

Ryan breathed.

As he repeated the process, in and out, keeping it slow, he focused on pushing out his frustrations and inhaling positivity. He'd never gone in for meditation before the attack. But in the hospital, his respiratory therapist, a retired cop who'd taken up the gig to keep from getting bored, had convinced him that it helped.

And when he could quiet his mind enough to try it, it did. The problem for Ryan Hernandez was that his mind was usually a series of bouncing, disconnected thoughts and fears that he couldn't control, much less verbalize.

Would he ever rejoin the force? Would he ever walk again? Would he ever inhale without that brief, painful twinge so far back in his chest that it felt like a splinter had lodged there? Would Jessie grow weary of playing nursemaid and dump him once she'd given it the old college try? He couldn't quiet his mind back when he led a life of non-stop activity. How was he supposed to do it when he was trapped in this shell of a body with no outlet for his anxieties?

Still, as he sat propped up against the pillows of the hospital bed they'd had brought in, he tried to calm his thoughts. He tried to let go of the guilt he felt for lashing out at Jessie, who was only trying to help him. He tried to forget the fear he'd seen in Hannah's eyes when she walked into the room and found him sprawled out, helpless, on the floor. He tried to block out the memory of Jessie's ex-husband plunging a knife into his chest while he lay frozen in place, paralyzed by a drug that kept him awake and able to feel pain, but powerless to move.

He heard the blender in the next room and knew Jessie would be returning soon. He had to get a grip before then. He had to let her know he was sorry, that he appreciated what she was doing. He had to let her know that he understood that he couldn't do this again.

The road to recovery was going to be slow. Dr. Badalia had warned him that it might be weeks before he could get to the bathroom on his own. He'd said that targeting the new year to walk on his own normally again was realistic. It was September now. That meant that he was probably wheelchair-, walker-, and cane-bound for at least the next three months. The thought was unbearably depressing. And yet, that's the way it was.

Ryan had never been one to quit. No one had even expected him to graduate high school, much less finish near the top of his class at the police academy. No one had expected him to make detective at all, much less do it faster than almost anyone in department history. No one had expected him to lead the most highly regarded investigative unit in the LAPD before the age of thirty. Even he hadn't expected that after an ugly divorce, he'd find love again with a brilliant, gorgeous woman who kept him on his toes every day, if only figuratively for now.

*

Jessie took a deep breath and walked back in carrying a tray with a smoothie and a bowl of chicken noodle soup. She set it up in front of him and adjusted his bed so that he was fully upright. She wasn't sure if he wanted her to stay or go. He cleared the question up quickly.

"I'm...sorry," he said.

She pulled up a chair and sat down next to him.

"No, *I'm* sorry," she said quietly. "I know that this must be incredibly frustrating for you and I should have been here for you, not driving around the city on a wild goose chase. You didn't do anything wrong."

"Was sorry...for myself," he said as forcefully as his lungs would allow. "Not okay. Will...try harder."

She nodded.

76

"I get frustrated too," she admitted. "This is going to be hard, obviously more so for you than me. But for it to work, we need to make some hard choices. The reality is that Hannah and I need some help."

"Yes," he said, nodding in agreement.

That gave her the confidence to ask her next question.

"Are you willing to reconsider a night nurse, at least for a little while, until you're a little stronger?"

He nodded again, though he didn't speak this time. A single tear trickled down his cheek. Her heart ached for him.

"I know it's not ideal," she conceded. "But we'll get through it together, like we always have. Okay?"

His breathing was clearly labored so he offered her a thumbs-up instead of words. She leaned over and kissed him on the cheek, where the tear had settled.

In that moment she made them both a silent promise. She would solve this case fast. She had to, so she could get back to him, to Hannah, to her family, the most precious thing in her life.

CHAPTER FIFTEEN

"I'll take the bus home," Hannah said as Jessie pulled into the school driveway to drop her off. "I don't want you to have to stop in the middle of the case to get me."

"I'll be home by dinnertime," Jessie said, intent on making that promise a reality, no matter what. "What are we having?"

"It's a little something I like to call 'leftover surprise.'"

"Well, they can't all be winners," Jessie allowed.

"Hey, wait until you've tasted it before you talk smack," Hannah said as she hopped out.

With Ryan safe at home with Nurse Patty and in good spirits when they'd left, both of them felt comfortable with a little teasing banter. Hannah was about to close the door when she seemed to think of something else.

"Now if I find this sexual slavery dude on campus, should I call you or Captain Decker?"

"Very funny," Jessie said, pulling out of the driveway.

She didn't say it, but Hannah's comment sent her into a spiral of thoughts about just how girls like Marla ended up in a fancy Pacific Palisades house, servicing the basest desires of men who used them and then tossed them away. She was tempted to call Decker to get an update but forced herself not to. He might not even have briefed Gaylene Parker yet. She had to give it a little time.

Instead, as she worked her way along the choked rush-hour streets, making the seventy-minute drive back to Otis Estate, where she planned to meet Karen Bray, she called Jamil Winslow. As she had anticipated, he was in and answered on the first ring.

"Winslow, Research."

"Hey, Jamil, how's your Monday morning treating you?" she asked.

"Busy, Ms. Hunt, very busy. I already have a few updates if you're interested."

"I'm always interested in what you have to share," she replied.

"Okay, how about we start with the victim's husband, Beto Estrada. You wanted to see if we could independently confirm his claim that he was home all night."

"Right," she confirmed. "Any luck?"

"Some," he said. "Based on a check of his GPS data, his phone never left the house after five p.m. and his car never moved from the driveway. But as we both know, that's not definitive proof of anything on its own. So I checked the cottage. Estrada is renting it from a management company. They use motion-activated security cameras on the exterior of all their properties. I don't know if Estrada was aware of that. In any case, I got them to send me the footage from Saturday night."

"Don't keep me in suspense, Jamil."

"It shows the same thing. There was no movement outside the cottage after five. So, either he was home all night or he's one stealthy middle-aged guy."

"Good to know," Jessie said. She didn't say it but she was secretly glad that Estrada seemed to be in the clear. It would have vastly complicated the credibility of the Marla tape if he had been lying about his alibi. "What else have you got?"

"I don't know whether this next bit is good news or bad news, but here goes. Tech has already done facial recognition on the camera footage from outside the main house during the party. Of the eight people you referred to us based on your research at the law firm yesterday—the ones who seemed like credible suspects based on their past criminal cases—all but two alibi out."

"How can you be sure?" Jessie pressed, as she zipped past an old pickup truck belching out dark clouds of exhaust.

"Because all six of them are clearly visible on camera, leaving the estate prior to the established window of death, from three o'clock to three fifty. We followed up using phone data to make sure that one of them didn't double back later and verified that none of them were on the estate property after three that morning."

"But you said that two were still there," Jessie reminded him. "Who?"

"One is the actor you interviewed yesterday, Rance Jensen. Because of the dampening technology used on the estate, we can't use his phone location data to determine where exactly he was. But the main house camera shows him arriving at the estate at nine forty-four p.m. and leaving at four oh-nine a.m. We're still trying to see if he was active on social media during that period. If so, it might help us piece together his whereabouts with more specificity."

"Good idea," Jessie said as she quickly switched lanes to avoid getting stuck behind a garbage truck. "So who's our final contender?"

"Percy Avalon, the singer."

"Ah yes," Jessie said, remembering the man who had claimed ignorance about an entourage member holding a woman in his hotel room against her will. "What's his story?"

"He showed up with a whole crew just after eleven p.m. The footage shows them all piling into a limo to leave around seven fifteen the next morning."

"That was just before Detective Bray and I arrived on the scene," Jessie said, dumbfounded. "The estate should have already been secured. Are you telling me these people were just allowed to leave?"

"According to the footage I'm looking at, they were met at the driveway by an officer with a clipboard, who took down some info from each of them—it looks like he's writing down the names on driver's licenses. But then he let them go."

"Wow," Jessie marveled in disgust. "These Westside cops definitely have a different way of doing things. Anything else?"

"Maybe one more thing. It doesn't have to do with your requests but I thought you might want to know. Around five forty-five a.m., there's footage of what looks like a catering staffer, a guy in his twenties, leaving through the main entrance. A few seconds later, a tall, middle-aged woman ran out after him. She caught up to him and looked like she was yelling at him. He said something back to her and she hauled off and slapped him. She hit him so hard that he was knocked to the ground."

Jessie had a sneaking suspicion who the slapper might be.

"You said the woman was tall and middle-aged," she noted. "Was she wearing a business suit with a scarf, with black hair tied up in a bun?"

"That's the one," Jamil said.

"Her name is Nancy Salter. She's Otis's estate manager. Can you do a check on her when you get a chance? I know we won't be able to track her location but we can at least look at her criminal history."

"On it," Jamil said.

"You're a lifesaver," Jessie told him. "Don't hesitate to pummel me with updates. I'm heading back to Holmby Hills now."

After hanging up, Jessie called Bray to update her on what Jamil had learned. When that was done, it still took her nearly an hour to finally get to the estate. Bray was waiting outside the gate. She didn't look happy.

"What's the problem?" Jessie asked.

"They're not letting me on the property. They say that Otis got a stay from a local judge, restricting any future searches without a warrant. I checked at the station. It's true. They've also reneged on the promise to provide the security footage from the entire estate. All we have is what they originally provided from the main entrance to the South House."

"These aren't the choices an innocent man makes," Jessie fumed, trying but failing to rein in her anger. "I've had just about enough of this guy and his games. I want this case solved."

"You're preaching to the choir," Karen said. "It's unbelievably suspicious. The problem is, now that they've informed me, I'm stuck. I can't proceed with anything here until the situation is resolved."

Jessie thought for a moment. When she replied, she was smiling slightly.

"If you're amenable, here's what I think you should do. Go back to Central station. See if you can get that warrant. Use Captain Decker if you have to. I think we'll have better luck if we go to a judge we deal with regularly, rather than one who might be in Otis's pocket. Besides, by then Jamil may have locked down more details on where Rance Jensen and Percy Avalon were that night. If not, maybe you can think of some avenues of inquiry that didn't occur to him."

"All that sounds fine," Karen said, a curious look on her face. "But where will you be while all this is going on?"

"You know, I think you're better off if I don't tell you."

"You're not going to do something crazy, are you?" Karen asked.

"I guess that depends on how you define crazy," Jessie told her. "I'm not an LAPD employee. I'm just a private citizen consulting for the department. As such, I'm not bound by the same rules as you. And I'm not inclined to let some entitled, self-satisfied billionaire determine how I can investigate this murder. Milly Estrada deserves better than that. She deserves justice. And I'm going to get it for her."

Karen didn't respond to that other than to smile. She got in her car and backed out of the driveway. As she pulled away, she lowered her window.

81

"Let me know if you need me to bail you out," she shouted as she drove off.

Once she left, Jessie parked her car half a block down the road, walked back in the direction of the main gate, and sat on a bench near some bushes in the park across the street. Ten minutes later, a dry-cleaning service van pulled up. The gate opened and the van headed up the driveway.

Jessie got up from the bench and casually jogged across the street. She darted by just before the gates slammed closed. The sound clarified one clear thought in her head.

No turning back now.

CHAPTER SIXTEEN

She tried to act casual.

It was hard, considering that she had to make her way up a quarter-mile-long driveway to a massive mansion that she knew was at least partially monitored by 24/7 security. She expected personnel to show up at any second and kick her out.

When she got up to the roundabout in front of the house, she discovered why that hadn't happened. Security had their hands full. There were already lots of people milling about. In addition to the dry cleaner, there were landscapers putting equipment back in a truck, several people doing work on a nearby stone fountain, and someone carrying pool equipment from a van around the side of the house.

Jessie decided that might be her best bet. If she approached the place from the side, she'd be less likely to attract attention than just wandering up to the front door. So she jogged after the pool guy as nonchalantly as possible.

"Hey," she called out when she was close enough that only he could hear her. "Need a hand? It looks like something's going to drop at any second."

The guy turned around. He was in his fifties with gray hair and leathery skin that had clearly spent many years in the sun.

"Sure," he said, offering her an unwieldy plastic hose. "I'd never turn down an extra hand. Is this a new policy?"

"What do you mean?"

"This is the first time a staffer has ever offered to help me with anything," he said. "No offense, but your bosses aren't exactly worker-friendly."

"None taken," Jessie said, throwing the hose over her shoulder. "I'm actually a peon too, and a new one, so I'm right there with you. Do you clean the pool every Monday?"

"Yep. And Fridays too. Those are pre-party prep days. Mondays are for post-party cleanup. They're the worst."

"Why do you say that?" Jessie asked, moving the hose closer to her face as they passed two employees walking by in the royal blue "$\mathcal{O}$" shirts that served as the Otis Estate uniform.

"You wouldn't believe the stuff I've had to fish out of the pool," he said. "The hot tub is even worse."

"What kind of stuff?"

"Trust me," he said, visibly shivering at the memory. "You don't want to know. Let's just say that with some of the things I've found, I'm surprised the health department hasn't raided this place. And there's no amount of chorine that could get me in that water."

They had reached the edge of the pool near the supply room. Jessie glanced around. There were about a dozen people lounging on chaises, most nibbling at pastries. Despite the early hour, a few young women were already in bikinis soaking up the sun.

"Thanks for your help," the pool guy said, extending his hand. "I'm Mike, by the way."

"Nice to meet you, Mike," Jessie said, shaking his hand but not giving her name. "I hope today's cleanup isn't too painful. I guess I better get back to my job too."

She grabbed a stack of towels and stacked them on her shoulder high enough to block her face from anyone she needed to avoid. Then she wandered over next to two youngish, model-looking women in robes sipping mimosas. She hoped they might be in a chatty mood.

"Anyone sitting here?" she asked them as she plopped down in the lounge next to them.

They exchanged disdainful looks before the blonder of the two replied.

"Is staff supposed to be chatting with guests like this?"

"Oh, I'm not staff," Jessie assured her as she laid out some of the towels and undid an extra button near the top of her shirt. "I just like to have a lot of towels for extra cushion. I hate it when these chairs leave lines on my skin. So are we back to normal yet or is all this police stuff still going on? I mean, I thought I was going to have a relaxing week on the West Coast and I get here to discover there's a frickin' murder investigation going on."

"I wouldn't sweat it," the less blonde woman said. "There's nothing major going on until the oiled-down Twister party tomorrow night. By then, I'm sure Jasper will have this whole thing taken care of."

"I'm sorry," Jessie asked. "Did you say oiled-down Twister party? That's a thing?"

"Sure," she said. "Jasper loves to update retro games. And if it gives him a chance to roll around with girls slathered in oil, you know he's gonna take it. You should check the itinerary. It's posted everywhere. There's all kinds of stuff coming up. I think he's got Strip Trivial Pursuit happening on Thursday."

"I don't really know Jasper," Jessie said. "I got the invite here from a friend of a friend. Is he cool? I'm not sure I'd be into playing any of that stuff with a fifty-something-year-old guy. It seems a little sketchy."

"He's no more pervy than your average middle-aged dude," the blonder one said. "But you don't really seem like the type who'd be into all of that under any circumstances."

Jessie pretended not to get the dig. She wanted to press harder on what they thought of Otis but feared it would come across as snooping, so she let it drop.

"I'll admit that's not how I usually spend my Thursday nights," Jessie said. "But I didn't come all the way from New York just to sit around for a week. I guess I'm game."

"That's the spirit," semi-blonde said.

"Hey, speaking of game," Jessie said, finally sensing they were comfortable enough with her to ask some real questions. "I heard I missed out on seeing some big names on Saturday. Is it true that both Percy Avalon and Rance Jensen were here?"

"Girl," replied super-blonde, "if you think those are big names, you're in for a shock. Those are just the guys who deign to mingle with the masses. Jasper keeps the really big names protected from the hordes in the West House, where we can't get at them."

"Like who?" Jessie asked conspiratorially.

"Ever heard of Senator Greg Johnson? Or Paul Gilliard, the Oscar-winning actor? Or Omar?"

"Who's that?" Jessie asked.

"Some Middle Eastern sultan or something. I can't pronounce his whole name so I just call him Omar."

"All those people were at the party on Saturday?" Jessie asked, trying to commit the names to memory.

Super-blonde's gossipy demeanor suddenly changed, as if she'd been busted in a lie.

"I'm not actually sure if any of them were here on Saturday. I didn't personally see them. Sometimes they hole up in the personal wing, away from us little people. But those guys are around all the time."

Jessie tried to hide her disappointment. The men she mentioned being around "all the time" at these parties weren't likely to sway Decker enough to agree to a full-court press on investigating their backgrounds. Semi-blonde, apparently sensing that Jessie felt cheated, leaned in.

"You were right, though. Those other guys were here that night. I saw Percy and I can personally vouch for Rance's attendance."

"What do you mean?" Jessie asked.

"A lady never tells," semi-blonde said, leaning back on her chaise.

"Yeah, but you're not a lady," super-blonde snapped before turning to Jessie. "What she means is that she nailed the guy."

Jessie forced the surprise on her face to come across as titillated more than ravenously inquisitive.

"Wow!" she exclaimed. "That's impressive. How much time did you get to spend with him?"

"Oh, you know," semi-blonde said, trying to sound laid-back, "we spent time together at two in the morning, three in the morning, had a bite to keep our energy up, then spent some more time together around dawn. You know what I mean?"

"How could she not know what you mean, Brittany?" super-blonde asked derisively. "You're not exactly maintaining the mystery."

"Sorry, I'm just proud. He's the biggest fish I've bagged so far this month."

"Haven't gotten to Percy yet?" Jessie asked leadingly.

"Maybe someday," Brittany said. "He's definitely around a lot. But he's usually got his boys with him. It's hard to break through that testosterone bubble when they're all together."

"Are you looking to claim a trophy?" super-blonde asked Jessie pointedly. "Because there's always someone available. But you're probably going to have to up your wardrobe game. Show a little more skin. I know you're older but you've got to put in the effort."

"I'm thirty," Jessie said.

"That's okay," super-blonde said. "Some of these guys like older women. But you've got to convince them that it's worth their while."

Out the corner of her eye Jessie saw Matilda, her guide from yesterday, walking toward the pool and decided it was time to pull up stakes.

"I'll think about it," she said, standing up and piling the towels back on her shoulder. "Maybe I'll go change now. The only problem is that I've got some scars."

"Where?" Brittany asked as she sat back up, way too intrigued.

"Everywhere, Brittany," Jessie told her. "Everywhere."

Before either woman could reply, she scurried away, passing right by Matilda, who glanced her way distractedly, and seeing nothing but a heap of towels, returned her attention to whatever task she'd been assigned. As she hurried away, Jessie noticed Cord Mahoney sprawled out face down on a lounge chair, seemingly passed out. He must have found his second wind at some point. He was shirtless and his skin was bright red. Jessie was briefly tempted to bump into him to wake him up so he didn't get even more burned. But she couldn't take the risk of him seeing her so she kept moving.

Jessie didn't look back until she'd rounded the corner. The back doors to South House were wide open. Realizing she might not have a better chance to get inside, she picked up the pace, hoping no one would notice her before she got in.

CHAPTER SEVENTEEN

She knew she looked suspicious.

Walking around inside with a bunch of pool towels on her shoulder would attract more attention than just trying pass as another guest. So she dumped them on an expensive-looking sideboard near the wall and veered immediately to the right, heading along the route she knew would take her to West House and the residential wing. She wasn't entirely sure what she was looking for but got the distinct impression whatever secrets needed uncovering would be discovered in the same part of the estate where Milly had died.

As she walked, she typed the names of the senator, actor, and Omar the Sultan into her phone so she wouldn't forget. It sounded like they might not have even attended the party, but it was worth checking into.

It also made Jessie wonder what other titans of politics, entertainment, and industry used the Otis Estate as their personal boys' club. And though she knew drawing too many conclusions was a risky proposition, the thought did occur to her that a sultan buddy of Otis's from a foreign country might speak a different language, as Marla had mentioned. There was no evidence to support the connections she was making, but that had never stopped her before.

As Jessie rounded the corner and headed down the hall that connected South House and West House, a slight, bespectacled male staffer with intrusive eyes passed by, give her a twice-over. She knew even before she reached the door to the residential corridor that she was busted.

She pretended to be oblivious, pulling open the doors and walking confidently, even as she heard a staticky hiss, followed by the guy's voice whispering into what she was sure was a walkie-talkie. The second she heard the doors close, she broke into a half-jog, bypassing the stairs that led to Otis's private wing.

She was more curious about the residential wing at the end of the corridor. The plastic tarps that had been set up for the mold remediation were still in place but she couldn't help wondering if there was a part of the residence that was still livable. Maybe a quick look around could reveal who'd stayed there recently.

She was almost to the end of the corridor when a booming voice called out from the other end.

"I wouldn't go in there. Black mold can have some nasty side effects."

Jessie stopped in her tracks and sighed. She recognized the voice. It was Nancy Salter. There was no way she could go any farther. Up until now, she could maintain the fiction that she was simply an LAPD consultant investigating a case and hadn't heard about the judicial stay, and that she just didn't want to bother anyone while she looked around to get some background for her investigation.

It was a clumsy, obvious lie, but it was technically defensible. However, if she continued to the residence, ignoring the clear directive of Jasper Otis's right-hand woman, she'd be in official trespassing territory. Reluctantly, she turned around.

Nancy Salter was already walking quickly toward her, with her bespectacled enabler in tow. Salter didn't look angry so much as energized by the chance to lay into Jessie. And yet, she kept her tone of voice conversational, almost accommodating.

"That's why they closed off the whole area and use air scrubbers," she continued. "Once they start cutting out the rotted wood, the mold is aerosolized. If that gets in your system, it can cause all manner of problems—breathing issues, infections. In really bad cases, people have had memory loss and hemorrhaging."

"Good to know," Jessie said, making a mental note to have Jamil look into the matter. "Maybe next time I'll bring my mask. When did the issue start again?"

"I'm terribly sorry, Ms. Hunt, but I'm afraid I'm not in a position to answer any questions at this time."

"Not in a position?" Jessie repeated, all doe-eyed and innocent. "That's an odd turn of phrase, Ms. Salter. Why on earth wouldn't you want to answer my questions?"

"Several reasons," Salter said, not at all moved by Jessie's dramatic turn. "First of all, you're trespassing."

"I'm not sure what you mean. You invited me onto the estate to investigate just yesterday. Why would you suddenly accuse me of trespassing the very next day?"

"That's the second reason," Salter said coldly. "As I'm sure you're aware, a judicial stay has been granted preventing any further visits without a warrant."

"I had no idea," Jessie exclaimed, pulling her hand to her heart. "Had I known that, I most certainly wouldn't have come."

"Detective Bray was informed. Are you not partnering with her on this matter?"

"Informally, sure," Jessie said. "But she works for LAPD and I'm just consulting. It's not like we're Cagney and Lacey or something."

Jessie saw the confused look on the face of Salter's assistant and suddenly felt much older than her thirty years. Salter clearly got the reference but wasn't amused.

"In light of your ignorance of the situation, we will merely have you escorted from the premises, rather than calling the authorities."

She nodded at her lackey, who muttered something unintelligible into his walkie-talkie. The arrogance was infuriating and, though she knew it was petty, Jessie couldn't help but take a poke of her own.

"I appreciate your restraint, Nancy. I wouldn't want to get on your bad side. I hear you have a brutal right hook, although maybe I'm safe. After all, I'm not a caterer."

She was happy to see Salter's eyes widen slightly. Realizing this might be the only opportunity to question the woman when she'd been thrown off a little, Jessie went in for an extra bite.

"Tell me, where were you on Saturday night between three and four, slugger?"

Salter had regained her composure even before Jessie finished the question.

"You are aware that I'm under no obligation to answer that…but I will. I was everywhere, Ms. Hunt. When it comes to Jasper's parties, I'm a bit of a whirling dervish, always in motion, always putting out fires."

"Put out any fires in Jasper's private wing that night?" Jessie wondered.

Nancy Salter smiled at her before answering. Her lips curled unnaturally, as if they were unused to that kind of movement.

"Not that I recall."

"That's odd," Jessie mused. "You seem like the kind of person who recalls everything."

"I do my best, but things can get crazy when trying to manage almost six hundred people."

"I'm sure," Jessie said consolingly. "Maybe checking the location data on your phone would help refresh your memory."

"Maybe," Salter said. "Unfortunately, as Jasper mentioned, the digital dampening net we employ on the property makes that sort of thing impossible."

"Oh, right. I forgot about that," Jessie lied. "That's really unfortunate for us law enforcement types. If not for that, we might have Ms. Estrada's killer in custody already."

The doors at the end of the corridor opened and two burly men in suits, apparently graduates of the same security school as Ajax, walked quickly toward them.

"It appears that it's time for you to go now, Ms. Hunt," Salter said. "I'll leave you in the care of Alastair and Vincent. Good day."

She turned on her heel and was out of hearing distance before Jessie could think of anything good to say. Either Alastair or Vincent motioned for her to head back down the corridor. She did so, with one of them in front of her and the other behind.

As she returned to the main entrance of the house, Jessie felt an infuriating sense of helplessness. Despite all the smoke, there was no fire yet. She had no evidence definitively tying him to this murder. But Jasper Otis was guilty of something.

He clearly had an unhealthy, potentially criminal interest in underage girls. And if he wasn't Milly's murderer, why the hell did he seem to be covering it up? Was it just that he was so powerful that he didn't care how he looked as he bullied everyone in his way? Or was it something deeper? Was he hiding some secret so nefarious that it was worth weathering whatever suspicion he faced to keep it hidden?

Either way, it was a tactical mistake. If he'd done his research on Jessie, he would have known she didn't back down. Not from serial killers, not from corrupt cops, not from drug cartels. And certainly not from pedophile billionaires.

He didn't know it yet, but she was coming for him.

CHAPTER EIGHTEEN

Hannah focused in on her target.

Yes, she'd been kidding when she told Jessie that she'd keep her eyes out for scummy guys with business cards looking for potential sex slaves. But the truth was she didn't need to, because she'd already been approached. Just not by a guy.

It was only her third day on campus when a fellow senior had approached her and asked her if she'd ever considered "going on dates." Hannah had misinterpreted the question and said she wasn't into girls (though she had no idea if that was really true or not).

"I don't mean that kind of date," the girl, who called herself Elodie, had said. "There are older guys who will pay good money to be with a high school girl, especially if she can prove she isn't eighteen yet."

Hannah, who knew girls back at her old San Fernando Valley high school who'd done porn, wasn't shocked that a variation on the sex work theme existed at this school too. Of the many things she'd seen and been through, learning about an underage prostitution ring didn't make the top five.

At the time, she'd politely declined. She wasn't interested, but not knowing who had the power at her new school, she didn't want to alienate anyone. Elodie hadn't seemed too broken up about it. Hannah got the sense that getting candidates for this gig was a volume business.

"Reach out if you change your mind," Elodie had told her before moving on.

That's what Hannah was about to do. She had no idea if this was a run of the mill teen hooker ring or if it might be part of the larger sex trafficking operation that had Jessie so upset. She aimed to find out.

She walked over to Elodie Peters, whose last name she had learned earlier that morning. The girl was sitting at a picnic table under a tree, scrolling through her phone. Hannah let a bit of self-doubt creep in. She couldn't help but wonder if what she planned to do was a violation of her promise to Kat.

Their deal was that Kat wouldn't mention the drug dealer confrontation if Hannah agreed not to take any more unnecessary, dangerous risks. But this wasn't an unnecessary risk. It wasn't pushing boundaries just for the sake of seeing what would happen.

If talking to Elodie got her a lead that helped her sister with a case that was clearly worrying her, it seemed more than worth it. Moreover, if it in some way saved young girls in trouble, then there wasn't even a question about whether it was justified. And if she happened to get a little thrill out if it along the way, there was no harm in that.

"Hey," she said, sitting down on the bench next to Elodie.

The other girl was also blonde, but far fairer than Hannah. Her skin was pale and freckles dotted her nose and cheeks. She was extremely skinny, with a boyish figure. Had Hannah not known she was a senior, she might have thought the girl was in middle school.

"What's up?" Elodie asked, looking up from her phone.

Hannah looked around, play-acting as if she was worried someone might overhear.

"I've reconsidered your offer," she whispered.

"What offer?" Elodie replied.

It was obvious that she'd been coached to be careful when someone else initiated this kind of discussion. Hannah leaned in even closer, trying to seem conspiratorial.

"You know, about the dates."

Elodie nodded as if this was the first she'd heard of it.

"What are you reconsidering?"

"I think I might be into it," Hannah said. "I mean, I already see older guys sometimes. If I can get more out of them than just a nice dinner and free drinks, that's something I might be interested in."

"What's your name again?"

"Hannah."

You're not a cop, are you, Hannah?" Elodie asked. "You know you have to tell me if I ask you that."

"I didn't know that," Hannah said. "I'm not exactly up on police procedure. But no, I'm not a cop. I'm just a girl who doesn't have enough cold weather clothes and wouldn't mind an occasional tanning session."

Elodie stared at her, trying to gauge whether Hannah could be trusted. Hannah looked back, intentionally projecting a mix of apprehension and excitement, though she felt none of the former and only a bit of the latter. She did her best to keep her disdain hidden. The idea that this silly teenage half-pimp could see into her soul was laughable. If she could, she'd already be running away screaming.

"Here's the deal," Elodie finally said, apparently convinced of Hannah's credibility. "Based on these guys' tastes, you might be a little old. When do you turn eighteen?"

"Next spring."

"That's cutting it close," Elodie noted. "But something about officially being underage makes a big difference to them, so that works in your favor. Plus, you have a lot of the qualities they like—tall, blonde, pretty, green eyes, athletic figure. A lot of the clients are foreign and don't see much of that in their countries. I could set up a meeting with my contact and see what he thinks. Interested?"

"I guess," Hannah said, keeping a bit of trepidation in her tone. "When?"

"How about after school today?" Elodie asked. "He could pick us up in the parking lot and drop us back afterward."

"Wow, that's fast."

"It has to be," Elodie said. "This isn't a small operation. There's a girl like me on half the campuses in the city, mostly the schools with girls who look like you and me. We bring candidates to our contacts, who decide if you're a good fit. They don't have time for girls who aren't sure. There are benefits if you do well—travel, that kind of thing. But you need to show Rico that you're committed."

"Rico?"

"That's my contact. He doesn't like it when I waste his time so I don't. I've brought him twelve girls since January and he's taken on nine. That's a solid record. I don't want to mess it up. So are you up for this or are you gonna chicken out when it gets real?"

"I don't chicken out," Hannah said, flashing her best "I'm in" smile. It seemed to work.

"Good. I'll meet you in the guest lot after school. Take this stuff," she said, handing over a plastic bag.

"What's in here?" Hannah asked.

"Some hair ties, barrettes, and a Catholic school–style miniskirt. After school lets out, put your hair up in pigtails and put the barrettes in. Wear the skirt. You want to sell yourself from the second he sees you. It's too bad you don't have braces."

"Sorry," Hannah said.

"That's okay," Elodie replied, not picking up on the sarcasm. "Just giggle and squirm a lot. Even Rico can be played if you know what he likes."

Hannah nodded. If there was one thing she was good it, it was playing people.

CHAPTER NINETEEN

"So Jensen's in the clear?" Karen asked in disbelief.

Jessie had just returned to Central Station and was sharing what she'd learned at the estate with Karen and Jamil.

"If Brittany is to be believed, then yes," Jessie answered. "And I didn't get the impression that she was making it up."

"Is this Brittany?" Jamil asked, directing their attention to an image on one of the four monitors on his desk in the research room.

Jessie confirmed that the woman, scantily clad and splayed out on a bed beside Rance Jensen, was her.

"Then that just about seals his alibi," Jamil said. "This is from Jensen's Instagram, posted at two fifty-seven a.m. on Sunday morning. I wasn't sure it was legit until now. But there are three others just like it that suggest he was quite busy at the time of the murder. Shall I show them to you?"

"That's okay," Jessie said. "I'll take your word for it. Any better luck on Percy Avalon?"

"Not yet," Jamil said. "I'm still searching but it doesn't look like he posted anything at all that night."

"Sounds like we may have to do some real-life, in-person questioning of the guy," Karen said, clearly more excited by the prospect of getting back in the field than poring over social media accounts.

"Agreed," Jessie said. "I think that should be our next stop. But before that, I was hoping something might have popped on Nancy Salter. The woman is definitely rougher around the edges than she lets on. And physically, I don't think she'd have much trouble breaking someone's neck, especially a person like Milly Estrada, who was much smaller."

Jamil shook his head.

"Afraid not," he said. "Her record is clean. The woman's never even had a parking ticket, though she has been sued a few times for creating an unwelcome work environment. Based on the way she clocked that caterer, I'd say that's an understatement. I'll keep probing though."

Jessie, who had really wanted an excuse to go after Salter, tried to hide her disappointment.

"What's that?' she asked, pointing at a monitor with a still frame from in front of South House.

Jamil glanced over to see what she was referencing.

"Oh, I used the main house footage to confirm when Millicent Estrada arrived at the party. It was pretty early in the evening, at eight forty-two."

He hit play and the screen unfroze to show Estrada walking from the parking lot to the main doors, where she waited briefly in line before entering.

"Play it back," Jessie requested.

This time she focused less on the woman's movements than on her presence. Milly Estrada had an elegance in motion that didn't come across in photos. As she walked, she held her head high, almost regally, as her dark, wavy hair bounced gently about her head.

Jessie could almost sense the excitement coming off her as she prepared to enter the party. Her gold blouse shimmered in the floodlights surrounding the house. Her long black skirt had a slit that rose provocatively to her upper thigh, revealing a toned leg that she must have worked hard to maintain.

Something about seeing her like that was incredibly bittersweet. Jessie was happy that this woman had decided to make a bold, fresh start, to reboot her life and pursue the passion that had been missing from it. And yet, it seemed that her embrace of this new, more exhilarating lifestyle led directly to the end of that life, to her lying half-naked, wet, and forgotten, with her proud, regal neck broken and limp.

Jessie felt impotent fury rise in her belly and reminded herself that it need not be impotent. She could do something about it. She had to. Pulling out her phone, she gave Jamil the list of big names that had been mentioned to her: Senator Johnson, actor Paul Gilliard, and Omar the mystery sultan.

"Based on Blondie-by-the-pool's walk-back, I'm not optimistic that we'll get any hits on these guys," she admitted. "But we should nail down their whereabouts anyway. And Jamil, I'd love it if you could do a full rundown on whoever this sultan is—background, assets, anything out of the ordinary."

"Am I looking for something specific?" Jamil asked, his interest piqued.

"You'll know it if you see it," she said.

"Are we off to see Avalon then?" Karen asked, hoping to keep things moving.

"In just a few," Jessie assured her. "I just have talk to Captain Decker about another matter. Meet you at the car in ten?"

After Karen headed out, Jessie went in search of Decker. The mention of the sultan reminded her that she'd given the captain more than enough time to fill Detective Parker in, give her the tape, and get an update.

With nightmarish visions of girls even younger than Hannah being tied down and blindfolded filling her head, she quickly walked to his office but found it empty. Returning to the bullpen, she saw Detective Alan Trembley over in the HSS section and approached him. Trembley was a solid detective, if perhaps a bit too much of an eager beaver.

"You seen Decker lately?" she asked when she reached his desk.

"That's the greeting I get?" he said, feigning offense. "No 'hiya Trembley'? No 'how's it going?' No 'can't wait to work with you again'?"

She gave him her best "not now" glare and tried again.

"Hiya, Trembley. How's it going? Can't wait to work with you again. Where is Captain Decker?"

Sensing that she wasn't in a playful mood, he answered directly.

"I think he went to Vice."

"Thanks, Trembley," she said sweetly. "Talk soon."

She hurried down the back hall. Vice had a dedicated section of the bullpen, but its leader, Detective Gaylene Parker, had a second, smaller office at the far end of the building. It was designed as a place where sensitive material could be reviewed and discussed without prying eyes or ears.

She was halfway down the hall when she saw Decker returning in her direction. They made eye contact and she immediately knew something was wrong. He stopped in his tracks with a guilty look on his face. That only made her move toward him faster.

"What the—?" she started to say as he held up his hand and shook his head.

"Join me in the courtyard, please," he said quietly.

She followed him outside and to an isolated corner where no one else could approach them without being seen well in advance.

"What is it?" she hissed, preparing herself for whatever bad news she knew he was about to share.

"I may have screwed up," he said.

"What does that mean?" she asked, doing her best to keep her anxiety in check.

"Yesterday, after you played the audio for me, I dropped the thumb drive in Parker's secure locker."

"Oh god," Jessie muttered, already sensing where this was going. "Please don't tell me what I think you're going to tell me."

"I left her a voicemail letting her know to check it first thing this morning," he said, pressing forward. "I was completely generic, other than to say it was high priority. When she got in this morning, the locker was busted open and the drive was gone."

Jessie knelt down and hugged her knees. The things she wanted to say to Decker wouldn't just get her kicked off the case, they might get her arrested, so she stayed silent, waiting for the wave of rage to pass. Instead it lingered like a rain cloud that wouldn't move on.

"This is on me," he said. "I don't know how it happened but clearly my house isn't in order. Someone knew you had the file and gave it to me. Someone knew I gave it to Parker. Someone in this station took it. I don't know where the leak is but I'm going to plug it. I'm going to personally review security footage alone in my office when we're done here. I'll check every second from when I dropped the drive in that locker until Parker called me back. I'll check the entry logs. I'll check access card swipes."

"Captain," Jessie said, her head still down. "Obviously someone with resources didn't want that file investigated. We can both make educated guesses about who that might be. Almost no one knew about it and yet it was taken. Do you really think the people responsible for that don't have the power to cover their tracks? We're never going to find out who did it."

"You let me worry about that. I've talked to Parker and given her the essentials about the interview with Marla. She said she's heard rumors about this kind of thing for years but has never been able to pin anything down. She's going to open some doors—quietly. This isn't over, I assure you."

"I feel like this girl was reaching out to me for help," Jessie said. "And I've failed her."

"You didn't fail her, Hunt. If anyone did, it was me. But truth be told, she may be past saving. That interview was from 2017. The chances that 'Marla' is still alive aren't great. But that doesn't mean we can't help the other Marlas out there."

"How?" Jessie asked.

"I don't know yet but I'm going to run this to ground. You stay focused on the Estrada case. That's the one thing you have some control over right now."

Jessie nodded. He was right. There was nothing she could do about Marla right now. But she *could* find Milly Estrada's killer. If fate was just, maybe the two would intertwine at some point. She stood up.

"I need something," she said, knowing full well that there was no better time to make a tough demand of Decker. "Otis got a judge to grant a stay on our search warrant for the estate. I need it lifted."

Decker scratched his head.

"That's not going to be easy," he warned.

"I don't care, Captain. It's a goddamn crime scene. We're entitled to access. Who the hell ever heard of a private citizen being able to prevent law enforcement from investigating the site of a murder? I know the guy is powerful, but the stay is ridiculous on its face. Shame the judge. Go to the press. Do whatever you have to do, but I want access to that house. There's something fishy going on there and I shouldn't have to fake being a pool girl to prove it."

"I'll see what I can do," he said noncommittally, purposefully not asking about the pool ruse.

"No excuses, Captain," she said more directly than she'd ever spoken to him before. "You owe me."

CHAPTER TWENTY

Jessie seethed silently.

Even though Karen Bray didn't know her very well, she clearly had the good sense to realize that Jessie wasn't in a chatty mood just now. So she silently drove to Percy Avalon's house, leaving Jessie alone with her thoughts.

No matter how hard she tried, she couldn't get Jasper Otis out of her head. His smarmy, smiling face kept popping up like a billionaire whack-a-mole.

Though she couldn't prove it, he was almost certainly behind the Vice locker break-in. That meant he'd effectively quashed the only evidence that he might be a sex-trafficking pedophile. And now he was in the process of quashing a murder investigation.

He'd prevented them from executing a search warrant. In addition, multiple people had apparently come forward in the last day, volunteering to be witnesses who could verify that Otis was around them at the time of the murder. There were so many, in fact, that it seemed the man was rubbing Jessie's nose in it. Either he was lucky to have so many friends around or he paid very well for alibis.

There was no camera evidence tying him to the scene of the murder because there were no working cameras in his personal residence, the area where they could actually prove useful. There was no GPS data available because his whole estate was blanketed in a dampening net. A call to Len Fustos, the medical examiner, had confirmed what she'd feared—because of the shower water and the unprecedented disturbance and cleaning of the murder scene, there was no useful DNA or fingerprint evidence. They had nothing on the guy. Not a thing.

Her phone alarm buzzed, pulling her out of her pity fest. It was a reminder to call Nurse Patty to see how Ryan was faring. The fact that she wasn't there to make that determination for herself left a lump of powerful regret in her throat, one she swallowed down hard as she called. Patty picked up the first ring.

"How's it going?" Jessie asked.

"Not too bad," Patty said. "His appetite has been solid and he really pushed hard during rehabilitative therapy. They went for an hour, double what the therapist usually starts out with."

"That sounds like Ryan," Jessie said. "Can I talk to him?"

"He's actually sleeping right now. He was pretty wiped out after the rehab and the subsequent bath. It's already been a full day."

"Okay," Jessie said, disappointed. "Well, keep me posted please, Patty. Hannah will be home this afternoon and I'll be there by dinner. The night nurse should be arriving at five."

She hung up and tried not to think about Ryan needing assistance getting in the bath. She knew he found it humiliating and didn't like anyone to help him but her. But she had to get over the guilt. If this new normal was going to work, it would have to be a team effort.

"How's he doing?" Karen asked. "If I'm not intruding."

Jessie shrugged.

"It sounds like he's putting in the effort. So how's he doing? I choose to believe 'well.'"

They were quiet the rest of the ride to Percy Avalon's. The singer lived in a section of the Hollywood Hills above West Hollywood, just north of the famed stretch of Sunset Boulevard that included legendary clubs like Whisky a Go Go, The Viper Room, and The Roxy.

Karen took the turns of the narrow, winding uphill roads fast, as if she was trying to generate some adrenaline after the slog of spending all morning doing boring deskwork. Jessie clung to the door grip handle, trying not to come across as a wuss, even though she feared they might tumble off a cliff at any moment.

When they arrived, Karen pulled up halfway onto the curb to protect her car from drivers like herself. They got out and walked up to Avalon's gate. Though it suffered by comparison to Jasper Otis's place, this home was, by any normal measure, impressive.

It was designed to look like a modern version of a medieval castle. There was something slightly cheesy about it, but once she got past the conceit, Jessie thought the actual home was quite charming. It seemed to be winking at itself, with a small, easily traversable stream that served as a moat, intricate spires, and what looked like a bell tower.

When Karen pushed the buzzer by the gate, it opened almost immediately, without anyone asking questions. She looked over at Jessie, who shrugged and led the way in. They crossed the stream using the small drawbridge and walked up stone steps to the huge metal doors. One of them was half open.

Karen poked her head in, and seeing no one, grabbed the large knocker attached to the door and banged it, inducing an echoing clang. A minute later, a barefoot, middle-aged guy in sweatpants and a T-shirt came to the door. He was wearing sunglasses and his silvery hair dangled past his shoulders.

"Ladies?" he said. "What can I do for you?"

"We're with LAPD, here to talk to Percy Avalon," Karen said, pulling out her badge. "Is he around?"

"Wild," the guy said, taking off his sunglasses to reveal red-tinged, clouded eyes that weren't surprising considering the scent emanating from him. "Yeah, he's out back by the pool. You wanna say hi?"

"I think we'd like that very much," Jessie said, smiling pleasantly. "Can you lead the way?"

"Sure," he said, apparently not at all troubled by having law enforcement show up unannounced. "Is everything cool?"

"Unfortunately, no," Jessie told him. "We're investigating a crime and we're hoping Percy can help us out. Do you work for him?"

The guy laughed wheezily at the question.

"You could say that," he said. "I'm Wally, by the way. I'm what you might call a procurer of items."

"What kind of items?" Karen asked.

"Oh, household necessities. Everything from toilet paper to kombucha."

"I see," Karen said, not pressing him on what other necessities might be on the shopping list.

They passed through a long central hallway, lined with paving stones, into a more modern living room with a wall-sized TV screen at one end, and finally to a sliding door that led outside. When it opened, they were enveloped by the sound of piped-in music, which Jessie assumed was Avalon's. She wasn't a connoisseur of his work. They walked up a set of stone stairs that opened onto a kidney-shaped pool with a waterfall and a water slide.

There were half a dozen people, all men, spread out around the pool. Some were in chairs, others on chaise lounges. One guy was seated at the mouth of the slide, dangling his feet in the water. Jessie was pretty sure that at least some of them were band members. Beer bottles were strewn about and two of the guys were sharing a bong.

Jessie and Karen ignored them and walked over to the man sitting in a chair in the shade of an umbrella-adorned deck table. He was dressed only in red swim briefs, a bold choice under any circumstances, but especially when the temperature was hovering in the mid-sixties. His salt and pepper chest hair looked like a bird's nest and most of the skin on his back and arms was covered in tattoos. His gray hair was even longer than that of his procurer, Wally.

They both recognized him as Percy Avalon, lead singer of Humbert Humbert, a hugely successful rock band from the early 2000s that still attracted solid crowds on their seemingly endless tours. Avalon was known as a wild man in the band's heyday, repeatedly arrested on drunk and disorderly charges. He once even got into a fistfight with the lead singer of another band backstage at the Grammys. Both men were arrested, though they were each allowed to perform onstage before being carted off. In more recent years, Avalon seemed to have mellowed, at least until the recent false imprisonment charge that Milly Estrada got knocked down to accessory and time served.

"Uh-oh," Avalon yelled over the music as he saw them approaching. "Professionally dressed women in my house? This can't be good."

"Hello, Mr. Avalon," Karen said loudly when she was close enough to be heard. "I'm Detective Bray of the LAPD. This is Jessie Hunt, a consulting profiler for the department. We need to ask you a few questions about the party you attended on Saturday night."

Avalon stretched his arms out in the air as he closed his eyes tight. He seemed to be concentrating.

"What party did I go to Saturday, boys?" he shouted to the collective group.

"Jasper's," called out the guy sitting on the water slide.

"I thought that was Friday night," Avalon countered.

The guy in the chair closest to him shook his head and, even though he was only feet away, bellowed his reply. Jessie winced at the volume of his voice.

"Friday was Jenna's Malibu thing," he barked. "Remember, we jammed on the beach until the neighbors called the cops."

"Oh yeah," Avalon remembered, turning his attention back to Karen and Jessie. "It seems some people don't like impromptu concerts outside their window at two in the morning—lame. So what about Jasper's party?"

"We're looking into the death of Millicent Estrada at the party that night," Karen announced loudly. "We understand that you knew her, that she was your attorney, in fact."

Avalon sat up straight in his chair.

"Shut the music off!" he yelled to no one in particular. "Shut it the hell off!"

A second later, everything went quiet.

CHAPTER TWENTY ONE

"Milly's dead?" he asked, sounding serious for the first time.

"I'm afraid so," Jessie said, watching him closely. "She was murdered at the party."

Avalon lowered his head, as if he might be saying a silent prayer. When he lifted it again, he looked somber.

"That's a real bummer, man," he said quietly. "She was a cool lady, super tough. You know she helped me out of a jam a little while back. I could have spent some serious time behind bars if it wasn't for her. And she helped my boy Wavy Davey over there too. She got a four-year sentence knocked down to just over a year, didn't she, Davey?"

Wavy Davey, the guy sitting on the water slide, nodded. He didn't look nearly as appreciative as Avalon.

"Yeah," Avalon said. "He's my roadie extraordinaire. Things just weren't the same on tour without him. Nobody else knew how set up my snacks right."

Jessie tried to get him focused back on the case. The guy seemed easily distracted.

"So you didn't have any animosity towards Milly for not preventing you from spending time in jail while you awaited trial?" she asked.

"Nah, man. She didn't have control over that. And she got me a sweet private cell—said I was at risk in general population. She was a smart lady."

"So where were you that night?" Karen asked.

"Oh jeez, it was a long night. But we spent most of it by the fire pit, hanging out and doing an acoustic set. How long were we out there, boys?"

At the mention of the fire pit, Jessie suddenly realized that this was the same band that one of the party girls sipping mimosas on the patio yesterday had referenced listening to. Apparently the girl was too young to know that the band was called Humbert Humbert and not Hubert Humphrey. It seemed that Jessie wasn't quite as culturally illiterate as she'd feared.

"We probably jammed non-stop from about one a.m. until after four," the guy sitting next to him said. "We only stopped because

Jasper's house lady shut us down, said the cops were going to show up."

"Oh jeez," Avalon said, hitting himself in the forehead. "I remember that. I thought there were neighbors complaining about the noise, like at the beach house in Malibu. You don't think it was because of Milly, do you?"

"That's very likely," Karen said. "So can anyone verify this jam session outside of your friends here?"

"That shouldn't be a problem, madame detective," Avalon replied laconically. "You could probably check with the couple dozen chicks that were with us. Lots of them were shooting video on their phones. Find them and it should show what was up."

"I think we'll do that," Jessie said before turning her attention to the roadie extraordinaire. "Hey, Davey, can you come over here? I have a few more questions for you but I don't want to yell."

Wavy Davey pushed himself off the slide into the water and swam over. While they waited, Karen asked one last question.

"What do you think of Jasper, Mr. Avalon?"

The singer smiled, revealing yellowed, tobacco-stained teeth.

"He's solid—knows how to throw a party *and* how to party. That's a special skill set."

"He ever seem to party too hard?" Jessie probed.

"Is there such a thing?" Avalon asked seriously.

Wavy Davy grunted as he pushed himself out of the pool. Someone tossed him a towel as he stood up. Karen pointed back to the house and he followed the women back down to the living room at the bottom of the stairs.

Wavy Davey looked like a guy used to living his life on the road. His skin was blotchy and his stubble was patchy and uneven. His hair was thin on top but long in back, resting on his shoulders in a thick, oily gray clump. He pulled a T-shirt on over his pale, ample belly.

"Have a seat," Karen said. "What's your full name, Davey?"

"David Dwight Pasternak."

"But you prefer Davey?" she asked.

"It's not really a matter of prefer," he said. "Percy started calling me Wavy Davey so that became my name."

"I'm wondering, David," Jessie said, hoping to throw him off a bit with the proper name, "were you as happy with Milly's legal efforts on your behalf as Percy was?'

He shrugged.

"She did the best she could, all things considered," he answered.

"That doesn't sound like a full-throated endorsement," she noted.

"I mean, what do you want from me? I spent fourteen months behind bars. I didn't get any private cell either. It was rough. That wasn't her fault but I'm not going to pretend I was psyched to be there."

"Well, David," Karen said, following up on Jessie's tack. "You *were* convicted of false imprisonment."

"Actually I confessed, on her advice."

"You're saying she coerced you into a confession," Karen pressed.

Davey looked at the both of them. The look of resignation that had been plastered on his face until now had been replaced with something closer to resentment.

"Listen," he seethed. "I'll deny this on the record, and none of it matters now because of double jeopardy, but I think we all know the truth. I never did anything to that girl. I took the fall for Percy. He was super high that night and he…couldn't perform with her, if you get my meaning. He was paranoid that she was going to spill that on social so he took her phone and locked her in the hotel bathroom. When his head finally cleared, he called me and I helped clean up the mess. I just didn't know the mess it would cause *me*, even after I got out of prison."

"What mess?" Jessie asked.

"It screwed me up pretty bad," he said, no longer making eye contact. "While I was in there, I was constantly worried about getting attacked or worse. I still have nightmares about the bars slamming shut at night. I was never a big drinker before. But since I got out, I've been doing whatever I can to numb myself. It hasn't been great."

Jessie felt some sympathy for him, but not enough not to do her job.

"So David," she said, "Milly pressured you into doing time for Percy, you're drinking heavily, and you end up at the same party as her. Did you run into her at all?"

"I don't know," he said.

"You don't know?"

He lowered his head, not answering. For a moment, Jessie thought he was clamming up. But when he lifted his head again, she saw that his eyes were wet. When he spoke, his voice sounded pinched with emotion, as if he was trying not to break down.

"I'd like to think I would never hurt Milly, or anyone. I've never gotten in any legal trouble before that hotel thing. But I don't remember much about that night. I got piss drunk. I passed out at some point.

When I woke up, I was lying by the gate to one of the petting zoo stalls. I was freezing and had ant bites all over me, which makes me think that's where I was all night. Someone had to wake me up so I didn't miss the limo the guys were taking back here."

"So you don't have any alibi at all?" Karen asked.

"Maybe you could check my phone?" he suggested. "Can't you use it to track where I was?"

Jessie and Karen exchanged exasperated looks.

"I wish," Jessie said. "Stay here for a minute, Davey."

She and Karen went to the far corner of the room where he couldn't hear them.

"I don't see how we don't bring him in," Karen began. "He's got motive and no alibi. *He's* not even sure he's innocent."

Jessie couldn't disagree on the merits. But that didn't stop her from making the case against it.

"If we arrest him, it's going to get out," she said. "Blabber will scream that the killer has been caught. And that will make it doubly hard to get that search warrant stay lifted. Otis will argue that we have no reason to go back to his place if we have a suspect in custody."

"Jessie," Karen implored. "We can't *not* arrest a suspect because it might hurt our chances of arresting a less credible suspect."

"I don't think Otis is a less credible suspect. I think he's just better at putting barriers in our way. Now, if you think that pathetic creature over there was responsible for this, I'll back you and we can take him in right now. But if you have any doubts, let's hold off. We can put a monitoring bracelet on the guy if need be. But we both know he's not going anywhere and I don't think he's a threat to anyone else other than himself."

Karen looked at her with an inscrutable expression that Jessie suspected she'd used many times on her husband and son. Finally she seemed to crack.

"Fine, we'll hold off for now. But he doesn't leave this house and we have him fitted with an ankle monitor. And if nothing new breaks with another suspect by this time tomorrow, we haul him in. I can't lose my job because I let a guy skate on your hunch."

"Thank you," Jessie said.

"Don't thank me just yet. I don't see any way to get at Otis."

"I may have an idea," Jessie replied. "But I have to pursue it on my own. Would you be willing to go back to the station and work with

Jamil, see if there's groupie footage of Humbert Humbert performing like Avalon said?"

"So I get the grunt work and you go on a secret mission," Karen said. "Can't you tell me anything about it?"

"Trust me, Karen, for your own safety, I can't say a word."

CHAPTER TWENTY TWO

Hannah thought she looked hot in a jailbait kind of way.

She gave herself a final once-over before running out to the guest parking lot to meet Elodie and hopefully, Rico. She had on the plaid miniskirt, which she couldn't kneel or bend over in without risking an indecency charge.

As Elodie had suggested, she'd put her hair in pigtails using the hot pink hair ties from the bag and added purple butterfly barrettes for good measure. She didn't have braces but had come up with what she considered an equally clever idea.

Over lunch she'd bought a pack of bubble gum, which she smacked repeatedly. It also let her blow big, sticky bubbles that would explode, allowing her to provocatively peel gum off her lips. The second Elodie saw her, she nodded approvingly.

"I like the way you think, girl," she said. "I may have to steal that one from you."

"Just trying to make a good impression," Hannah said, playfully jutting her hip out for emphasis.

"Don't get cocky," Elodie said, indicating for Hannah to follow her as she walked along the sidewalk. "Rico likes a little swagger in his girls, but not too much."

"Got it," Hannah said. "Where are we going, by the way?"

"He's picking us up around the corner, off school property and away from their security cameras. That's for our protection as well as his. We don't want to get called into the principal's office to explain this—got to be careful."

Hannah nodded in understanding. As they walked to the corner, she tried to plan out in her head how she could get Rico to reveal something incriminating. It was going to be challenging to show enthusiasm and get information without drawing any suspicion.

Plus she had to make sure to record the conversation without being discovered. That reminded her of the trick she'd thought of earlier in the day. She pulled out her phone. Elodie looked at her sideways.

"I'm just going to silence it," Hannah said. "So it doesn't ring in the middle of anything important."

Elodie nodded, agreeing that it was good idea. Quickly, Hannah went to the voice memo app, opened it, and turned off the screen again. Before she had time to say another word, a silver BMW with tinted windows pulled up at the corner just ahead of them.

"That's Rico," Elodie said. "Put on your babydoll face, girl. It's showtime!"

Hannah plastered on her best pout as the window rolled down. The person in the driver's seat was not what she'd expected. Somehow she'd pictured Rico as a burly, tatted out dude with a beard and bling. But the guy eyeing her was skinny, pale, and blond. He looked like he could be Elodie's older brother. She prayed that wasn't the case.

"Get in," he said by way of greeting as he put on a pair of sunglasses.

Elodie hopped into the passenger seat. For half a second, Hannah wondered if she'd made a horrible mistake that would result in Jessie finding her severed head in an alley. But it was too late to bail now so she slid into the backseat behind Elodie. The moment the door closed, Rico peeled out.

Hannah wasn't sure if she was supposed to introduce herself or wait. Deciding to let Rico take the lead, she snapped on her seatbelt and settled in, trying to keep the tingle of uneasiness in her gut from overwhelming her senses. She needed to stay alert and focused.

Rico spent the next few minutes silently weaving up and down streets and alleys. Hannah got the feeling that he'd done this routine many times before. Eventually he pulled into a two-story parking garage behind a strip mall and parked in an isolated spot on the first floor. He turned off the ignition, took off his sunglasses, revealing light, grayish eyes, and turned to Elodie.

"Wand her," he said to Elodie, who looked to the backseat.

"We're going to get out of the car for a minute," she said. "I need to wand you to make sure you're not wearing a wire or anything."

Hannah got out without complaint. Elodie ran the wand over her entire body. When she was done, she looked over at Rico, who still looked skeptical.

"Do the top," he said.

Elodie turned back to her.

"To be extra careful, he wants you to take off your top. You can keep your bra on but I have to check the underwire to see if there's anything hidden in there."

Hannah suspected that this exercise was as much about testing her boundaries as it was about checking to see if she was a cop. Despite the fact that she'd never undressed in front of a man before, she forced herself to act as if it was old hat, pulling off her top without hesitation.

Elodie inspected the bra, then gave Rico the thumbs-up. He nodded his approval.

"You can put it back on and get in," Elodie told her before getting back in the front seat.

As Hannah pulled her top back on, she saw that the other two were whispering intently. She decided that, with their attention off her momentarily, this was her best opportunity. As she slid back into the backseat, she "accidentally" knocked her backpack to the floor. Her stuff spilled out.

Rico looked back at her, irritated.

"Sorry," she said. "I'm just a little nervous. This'll only take a second."

She began shoving items back in the backpack. When Rico faced front again, she quickly opened the phone, hit the record button as she faked a cough, shut off the screen, and tossed it in the pack. She put it beside her on the seat and tried not to look at it while the others continued to whisper. Finally, Rico looked back at her again.

"Are you a cop?" he asked.

"No," she answered.

"Is your real name Hannah?"

"Uh-huh," she said.

"Show me your ID."

She fished it out of her wallet and gave to him. He looked at it briefly, then tossed it back to her.

"You turn eighteen in seven months," he said. "That doesn't give you much time."

"I'm a quick study," she said, trying to sound confident but not cocky. "If I know what's expected of me, I can hit the ground running."

Rico looked at Elodie.

"I told you this one had potential," she said.

"What kind of experience do you have?" he asked.

"Doing this for money?" Hannah said. "None. But I've had more than a few dates with older guys who were generous gift givers if I was liberal with my affection. Is this all that different?"

Rico scrunched up his face as if she was a complicated algebra problem he was trying to solve.

113

"I'm going to be straight with you, Hannah," he said. "I don't like to waste my time. You seem like you can handle yourself but if you're not down for what I tell you next, this is the time to bail. I drop you off back at the corner, we go our separate ways, and everyone lives their lives. No hard feelings."

Hannah nodded her understanding. He continued without asking for a reply.

"There's a lot of money to be made here. But if I lay this out for you and you say you're cool, and then back out, we will have a problem. The next step involves my boss, who talks to his bosses. They don't like hiccups. They don't like troublemakers. If they get upset with me, I get upset with you and that's no good for anybody. Am I making myself clear?"

"Crystal," she replied, embracing the shiver of excited trepidation spinning up her spine. It was a rare thing for her—to feel something intensely. She allowed herself to get lost in it for a second, to let the tingling sensation called fear consume her.

"Good," Rico said, snapping her out of it. "Here's the short version. I introduce you to my boss. He runs a full background check on you to make sure you're cool. It's way more than a wand and ID check. Some of our clients are big-time and they don't want any complications. Are you going to be able to pass a background check, Hannah?"

"Absolutely," she lied.

Any check they did would reveal not only that her adoptive parents had been murdered by her serial killer father, but that her half-sister was a criminal profiler who was cozy with the LAPD. That was likely an insurmountable hurdle to pass, which made it crucial to get as much intel out of this meeting as possible.

"Excellent," he said. "Assuming you're right, you'll be paired with a few of our more experienced, less...demanding clients. They'll give us reviews based on your skill and enthusiasm. Consider it a probationary period. Assuming that goes well, you'll be allowed to start dating whales. That's where the big money is. You might even be asked to spend a few long weekends at our Big House."

"Big House?" she repeated, trying to project girlish enthusiasm.

"Yeah—one of our sponsors provides a mansion with ocean views where girls can stay and get visits from clients. You'd have total run of the place—awesome media set-up, relaxing by the pool, unlimited access to whatever substances float your boat. It's a constant party."

114

Alarm bells began ringing in Hannah's head. Rico's description sounded a lot like the house that Jessie had mentioned last night. As keyed up as she was, it occurred to her that this would likely be her only chance to make sure she was on the right track before she'd have to submit herself to the kind of interrogatory gauntlet she knew she'd never pass. In that moment, she decided she had to go for broke.

"That sounds awesome," she said as giddily as she could. "And Elodie mentioned that there could be travel too?"

Rico shot the other girl a nasty look that seemed to suggest she'd spoken out of school. But when he turned back to Hannah, he had a big, clearly insincere smile on his face.

"Let me put it this way. If you prove you're a gamer, a lot of opportunities are definitely available. I know girls who quit school just months before graduating because they were raking in more dough than doctors and lawyers. But for that to be you, you've got to put in the work. Are you up for that?"

She pretended to take a second to think it over, then gave her most animated nod.

"I am," she said.

"Great," he said. "Then I'm going to drop Elodie off and you and I can go get started on that background check."

For the first time since she'd gotten in the car, Hannah felt a flicker of what she thought might be real fear.

"Now?" she said.

"Why waste time, right?" he told her. "The quicker you get the go-ahead, the quicker you can start making big bucks. And like I said, the clock is ticking for you. Once you're legal, your market value drops big time."

There was no way she could go with him. Once they did the background check and found out who she was, they'd immediately suspect her motives for agreeing in the first place. That severed head scenario suddenly seemed uncomfortably realistic.

"I would totally do it today," she said. "But I promised my mom I'd pick up my grandpa from chemo today. She usually does it but she had a double shift. If I'm not there when he's finished, they'll call her and I'll be screwed."

Rico stared at her silently for so long that she almost felt uncomfortable.

"This isn't good, Hannah. How can we count on you when you can't even do the first big meet that I ask for? And how are you supposed to do your client work if you have to pick up your sick grandfather all the time?"

"I'm sorry," she said. "Normally it's no big deal. I usually only have to get him about once a month. This just happens to be the day. But I didn't want to miss meeting with you. I just didn't know it would be more than a quick thing."

"We need to know you're reliable," he said.

"I am," she assured him. "Now that I know what's involved, I'll make it work. I really need this. I mean, the mansion and the travel sound great, but like I said, my grandpa's sick. This money could really help with all the medical bills. That's why you can count on me to be very popular."

He pondered that and seemed to find it compelling.

"What about tomorrow?" he asked.

"Tomorrow's perfect," she said. "I can totally make that work."

Rico glanced over at Elodie, who gave him a pleading look of her own. Her commission must be pretty nice to stick her neck out like this.

"Fine," he said. "Same time, same corner. Just you and me, got it?"

Hannah nodded.

"Thank you," she said.

They drove back to the corner near the school, this time taking a much more direct route. When they got out, Elodie leaned in through the passenger window to have a private word with Rico.

Hannah stepped back, as if she was giving them space. But the real reason was to get a clear look at his license plate. She would have liked to have snapped a photo of it but knew that was out of the question. Instead she silently repeated the combination of numbers and letters until Elodie joined her.

Rico pulled away and the two of them walked back to campus.

"Good job," Elodie said. "Other than the grandpa thing, I think that went well. And even that's not so bad."

"Why do you say that?" Hannah asked.

"You need money for his bills. That makes you desperate. They like desperate."

Hannah wondered how they'd like it when they got busted because of her. She couldn't wait to tell Jessie.

CHAPTER TWENTY THREE

Jessie was paranoid.

After what happened with the thumb drive and Detective Parker's secure locker, she had to assume her movements were being monitored. That's why she took forty-five extra minutes to get to her destination.

First, after they left Percy Avalon's castle, she had Karen drop her off near the busy intersection of Sunset and San Vicente. Then she made the short walk to the Book Soup bookstore a block away. She walked through the front door and wandered a few aisles, keeping an eye out for tails. When she was confident she wasn't in anyone's line of sight, she darted out the back door to the parking lot where she'd ordered her rideshare. The car was waiting.

She was dropped off several miles south at Cedars-Sinai Medical Center, a place she knew all too well due to multiple, injury-related stays. After getting out, she hurriedly navigated multiple halls, stairwells, and elevators, ultimately emerging just across from the Beverly Center shopping mall.

She joined the crowds there, exiting on the east side and hopping into another rideshare waiting for her on La Cienega Boulevard. Only then did she proceed to a house a block from her actual destination: the rented cottage of Beto Estrada.

Once she got out, she walked slowly, eyeing every car that passed by. No one slowed down or gave her a second glance. Still, she cast nervous looks over her shoulder as she walked up to the front door and knocked. It took much longer than she liked for him to respond.

"Go away," he said through the door. "You can't be here."

"We need to talk, Mr. Estrada," she insisted.

"It's not safe—for either of us."

"I took precautions getting here, Mr. Estrada. I wasn't followed. But if someone guesses that I was coming here and they see me on your front porch, all that effort is for nothing. Please let me in."

There was no answer. Jessie began to think that he'd simply walked away and planned to ignore her presence.

"Go the side gate," he said. "I'll unlock it."

She darted over quickly to the wooden gate. While she waited, an unpleasant sense of guilt overcame her. It wasn't until she had decided to come here to see him that she started to think about taking evasive measures. And even then, she hadn't considered the extent to which he might be freaking out.

At least she had the support of the LAPD behind her as she fought the power of Jasper Otis. Beto Estrada might be a successful attorney, but ultimately he was just a private citizen going up against a billionaire with unlimited resources and apparently, few scruples. He must be terrified.

When Estrada got to the gate, he opened it just enough for her to slide through. Without a word, he led her to the small backyard.

"Wouldn't you rather go inside?" she asked.

He shook his head.

"I don't think it's secure," he said. "Besides, you won't be staying long. Why are you here?"

Even before she'd arrived here, Jessie suspected that Estrada would be reluctant to sign on to what she had in mind. Looking at him now—exhausted, grief-stricken, and even more suspicious than she was of everyone around him, the chances seemed almost impossible. And yet she had to ask.

"I need you to go on the record about Otis. I need to you to say what you heard on that recording and reveal where you got it."

"Why would that be, Ms. Hunt?" he asked bitterly. "Could it be because you lost it?"

"Why do you say that?" she asked, taken aback.

"Because of this," he said, pulling a thumb drive out of his pocket. It looked like the same one he gave her yesterday.

"Is that what I think it is?"

He nodded.

"I came home early today," he told her. "I couldn't concentrate at work. When I went into my office, I found it on my desk, along with this note."

He handed over a small piece of paper with a briefed typed message: *WE KNOW.*

Jessie's heart sank. She understood why Estrada was so freaked out. She couldn't blame him. But even as she felt sympathy for his plight, her mind was processing her own.

As evidence, the note was mostly useless. She could collect it, but he'd already handled it, compromising it. She doubted that whoever had left it was foolish enough to leave personal traces anyway. Besides, the paper and type were pretty standard. There was no way to distinguish where it came from. Worse, the statement "we know" was general enough that, even if they found the culprit, it would be hard to charge them with anything more than breaking and entering. It wasn't technically a threat.

"We can check the security footage," she offered lamely. "Maybe that'll reveal something."

"That's not the point, Ms. Hunt, and you know it. I gave this drive to you yesterday for safekeeping and a day later I get it back, completely wiped clean, by the way. This is a clear message to me. Shut up or you end up like that detective. I hear it loud and clear."

Jessie knew it was pointless to argue with him. He was right. She was supposed to be someone he could count on and she'd failed him. Worse, she couldn't promise him that it wouldn't happen again. She motioned for him to follow her to the corner of the yard, far from the house. When he got there, she spoke quietly.

"You're obviously already aware that if they broke into your house to leave the drive, they've likely bugged it too. I wouldn't be surprised if they did the same at your office. They've likely geo-tagged your car as well. I wouldn't trust that your phone is secure either."

"You're really bucking me up here," he replied sarcastically, his shoulders sagging notably.

"I just want to be straight with you, Mr. Estrada. Clearly, we underestimated the resources and commitment of the people who want to keep this secret. That's on me. But I can still help you."

"How?" he asked beseechingly.

"I'm friendly with an FBI agent. I can make one call and get you put in protective custody."

"I'm not testifying," he insisted.

"This isn't about that. We'll find a way to protect you, whether it's formally part of the WITSEC program or not. We can get in a car now and go to his office."

He shook his head.

"You really think they couldn't find me? Come on, Ms. Hunt, don't be naïve. If I run, that will make them even more suspicious of me and more likely to take action. At least now, they see that I'm just leading my life, not acting as some kind of threat. If I run, they'll assume I've spilled, and they'll decide to eliminate me."

Jessie was desperate to convince him otherwise. It wasn't just about the case now. It wasn't just about his dead ex-wife. It was her fault that his life was in danger. He had put his trust in her and she'd failed him. She had to help him. She had to be straight with him.

"Mr. Estrada, there's nothing preventing them from doing that right now," she insisted. "At some point, they're going to decide that leaving you alive isn't worth the risk. That's when you'll have a car crash or suffer a drug overdose. They can make it look like an unfortunate accident. At least if you're under FBI protection, they have to think twice. They'd know that anything that happened to you then would put them at real risk. Either way, your old life is over. But if you come with me now, you might still have one."

Estrada stared off into the distance. Jessie didn't know if he was considering her idea or just remembering better times. Whatever it was, when he looked back at her, she knew immediately that he'd made the wrong choice.

"I can't," he said. "I have clients who need me. I have elderly parents and a sister with kids. They could be put at risk if I run. If I pretend none of this happened and just lead my regular life, maybe these people will leave me alone. Even if they take me out, that's where it ends."

Jessie nodded. She could tell there was no point in pressing him further.

"Give me your phone," she told him.

He handed it over without asking why.

"Here's my number," she said, adding it to his contacts. "If you change your mind, call me and ask me if Milly's personal effects are available to be picked up. Tell me where to have them dropped off. That'll be the sign for me to have a team pick you up immediately."

He looked at the number, then back up at her.

"Thank you," he said. "But I won't be calling. I'll walk you out now."

He led her back to the side gate, unlocked it, and opened it slightly.

"Think of it as your emergency SOS call," she pleaded. "Good to have it, even if you don't need it."

"That's sweet," he said resignedly. "But we both know you're already talking to a dead man."

She managed to wait until he'd closed the gate and she'd walked down the block to order her rideshare before losing it. She kicked a brick wall and even though her foot stung, she did it again. She wanted to scream and if she hadn't been on a residential street, she would have.

Jasper Otis was getting away with everything, including destroying the life of a man who'd just lost the woman he loved. She couldn't allow it. No matter what it took, she had to stop this guy.

She managed to calm down a little by the time her ride arrived to take her to Central Station. But as she sat in the back seat, turning everything over in her head, she felt the heat rising up her neck again. She seethed in vengeful silence.

CHAPTER TWENTY FOUR

By the time Jessie got to the station, she was ready to blow.

She stormed through the bullpen, heading down the back hallway to see what progress Detective Gaylene Parker had made on the sex trafficking case. If it wasn't sufficient, she was ready to ream the woman out.

But before she got there, she heard Karen Bray call out to her from the other end of the hall.

"Jessie. Didn't you hear me?"

"What?" she demanded, reluctantly turning around. "No. Can't it wait?"

"No. Jamil has some major updates. You need to come to Research."

Jessie forced herself to remain calm. Refusing to check out what Jamil had uncovered because she was focused on something else more pressing would only raise more suspicions. She needed to keep Karen from asking too many questions for her own sake. Besides, whoever had stolen that thumb drive was probably watching her closely too. If she barged into Parker's back office, it would be a pretty big tell as to what was on her mind.

"What has he got?" she asked, pretending everything was normal as she followed Karen back to Research.

"I'll let him show you," Karen said. "He did the heavy lifting. But I should warn you, you probably won't like it."

Of course not. Why should anything go my way today?

She followed Karen into Research, where Jamil was studying one of his monitors.

"What have we got?" she asked.

"You want the good news or the bad news first?" he asked.

"Your call, Jamil."

"Actually, now that I think about it, I don't know what you'd consider good or bad. So I guess it doesn't matter."

"Still waiting, Jamil," she reminded him, trying not to sound too testy.

"Right," he said sheepishly, getting down to business. "So as Percy Avalon apparently told you in his interview, he and his band *did* perform an extended impromptu set for much of the night. We've found multiple uploaded clips from at least at least five fans. Using those, I was able to piece together his timeline pretty conclusively."

"What does it show?" she asked.

"They started the set at twelve fifty-six a.m.," Jamil said, showing her a timeline he'd created on a second monitor. "They didn't wrap up for good until four oh-two a.m., though they did take several breaks in between. For most of the break time, they just hung around the area, doing a lot of...getting to know their fans. They did take two longer breaks, both about ten minutes. One was from one forty-seven a.m. to one fifty-eight a.m. The other was from two fifty-two a.m. to three oh-four a.m. In both cases, Avalon is off camera. That second break is technically within the window of death for Ms. Estrada."

"But..." Jessie said, leadingly, already sensing where he was going with this.

"But," he said, "the chances that Avalon could have stopped singing, gone all the way to Otis's private residence in West House, had some encounter with Ms. Estrada in which he removed her top and killed her, all before getting back to resume the set at three oh-four, are, to say the least, remote."

"There's more," Karen said. "Show her the footage when they picked back up at three oh-four a.m."

Jamil hit a button, and a time-stamped image of Percy sitting down on a stone bench began to play. The guy immediately made a crack about his aging bladder. He looked relaxed and untroubled. There was none of the anxiety or nervousness one might expect of a man who had just rushed back from breaking a woman's neck only minutes earlier halfway across the property.

Jessie had met people who were cold enough to react that way after committing murder, but not many. Plus he didn't look winded. She had to admit that while not a technical impossibility, the likelihood that Percy was Milly's killer seemed remote.

"What about Davey?" she asked.

"Ah, now that's another story," Jamil said, pulling up a new series of clips and walking her through them. "I used facial recognition from every social media video I could find to track his whereabouts. He's hanging out with the rest of the band and the entourage regularly until around one forty-five a.m."

Jessie pointed to a few of the images.

"It looks as if he's drinking in almost every clip you have of him," she noted.

"What's the significance of that?" Jamil asked.

"He claims he passed out at some point and woke up near the petting zoo."

"That's certainly possible," Jamil conceded. "Here's the last definitive image I have of him, in the corner of the screen while the band is playing at one forty-four a.m. You can see him get up and head off toward the west. He's stumbling and looking generally unsteady. After that, he completely disappears until we see him getting in the limo with the band as they leave the estate."

Jessie looked over at Karen, who was doing an impressive job of hiding her "I told you so" face.

"Did they put the ankle monitor on him yet?" she asked.

"Yep," Karen said, "about an hour ago. Even so, you know this means there's probably no way we can avoid picking him up."

"I know it doesn't look good," Jessie conceded. "But this could either sink him or reinforce his claim that he passed out. Either way, you promised we'd wait until tomorrow. You're not breaking your word, are you, Detective Bray?"

She said it with a playful lilt in her voice, but both of them knew this was a crucial moment for their current partnership and any future one. Jessie had to know where the woman's loyalties lay.

"I made a promise," Karen said. "I keep my promises. But remember you made one too. If we don't have somebody else in our sights by lunchtime tomorrow, we're taking him in, right?"

"Right," Jessie said reluctantly. "Then I guess we better find our guy, or girl for that matter. Jamil—any luck locking down Nancy Salter's whereabouts?"

He shook his head.

"I've been focused on this. That was next, along with trying to nail down how many senators, Oscar winners, and sultans were there. Any priority preference?"

Jessie thought about it.

"Let's start with Salter," she said. "That shouldn't take as long. Either we can lock in her movements or we can't. I have a feeling the others are going to require more bureaucratic hoop-jumping so let's hold off on those. Also, when you get a minute, I need you to check security footage from Beto Estrada's cottage this morning. Let me know if you see anything unusual after he left for work."

"Is that all?" Jamil asked, looking slightly exasperated.

"For now," she replied without pity. They all had major workloads. He'd get by. "Now if you both will excuse me for a few, I have to check in on another matter. Text if you need me."

"Is this check-in part of the whole 'can't tell me for my own safety' thing?" Karen asked.

"I can't answer that," Jessie said, smiling. "For your own safety."

CHAPTER TWENTY FIVE

Jessie didn't knock.

When she opened the door to the Vice Unit's back office, Detective Gaylene Parker, who was alone in the room, looked up, startled. But Jessie didn't apologize as she closed and locked the door and sat down opposite the head of the unit.

Talking to Karen and Jamil had calmed her down a little. She no longer felt the need to scream at Parker, which wouldn't have been very constructive anyway. But she wasn't in the mood to give her a pass either.

Parker's expression quickly changed from surprise to defensiveness. She clearly knew why Jessie was here and was girding herself for whatever onslaught was forthcoming. The woman crossed her arms and raised her eyebrows skeptically.

Gaylene Parker was somewhere in her mid-forties. A short African-American woman with an unfussy haircut and little makeup, she oozed veteran weariness. With the department for over twenty years, she'd worked her way up from street cop to detective to undercover vice to leading that unit. She'd even helped out HSS on occasion when they were short-handed.

Jessie always found her to be straightforward and competent with a no-nonsense attitude that was refreshing. But she was also extremely protective of her unit—both its people and its reputation. Even before she spoke, Jessie could see that she was on edge, aware that Vice might be blamed for yesterday's breach of security.

"How's it going, Gaylene?" Jessie asked, trying to avoid starting off adversarial.

"To be honest, I've been better, Jessie. I'm having one of those days. You know about those, don't you?"

"I do," Jessie assured her. "I'm having one of them myself. I was kind of hoping we might help each other out on that."

"What did you have in mind?"

"Well," Jessie said, treading carefully so as not to alienate a possible ally or adversary, "I know you're probably as frustrated as me about what happened yesterday. And I know Decker is trying to get to the bottom of it. In the meantime, I'm hoping you've had some success in finding leads on the case itself."

"I'm waiting for the part where you help me out," Parker said, not sounding especially accommodating.

Jessie could feel the irritation rising in her chest. She was the one who had secured the trust of a skittish potential witness. She brought in the Marla lead. She had a possible suspect using all his power to shut this down. What else was she supposed to do?

"I'm happy to run down any leads you have in mind," she said evenly. "I'm already in the thick of it with a potential suspect, one I assume Decker briefed you on."

"Here's the problem, Hunt," Parker said, apparently deciding they were no longer on a first name basis. "I'm trying to make sure my own house is clean. At the same time, I'm trying to investigate the circumstances of a detective's death, one from another division, without getting noticed. And I'm being asked to figure out if a mysterious, anonymous teenage girl was being trafficked by one of the most powerful men in the world. So my plate's a little full."

Jessie's reservoir of patience was just about full too. She took a deep breath before responding, hoping to take one last swing at amicability.

"I get your predicament, Gaylene. I don't envy it. But I've got a mess of my own, including a murder victim found at the home of that same powerful man, who knows I'm looking at him for the crime. I've also got a source who thinks, rightly, that his life might be in danger because the evidence he gave me was almost immediately stolen, likely at the behest of that same powerful man. So I've kind of got a target on my back. Maybe we could prioritize here. Decker said he's looking into the leak, which means you can set that aside. And if you let Internal Affairs handle Detective Shore's death, you'll be free to focus on the claims made in that audio file."

Parker shook her head.

"Decker doesn't trust IA right now," she countered. "That's why he has me looking into Shore, because we were both Vice. I knew him. I know the guys in that unit and how they think. But I have to tread carefully. So it's taking longer than I'd like."

"Okay, then hand over the Marla component to me and I'll look into it."

"You have time for that?" Parker challenged. "I thought you were conducting a murder investigation."

The question stung in a way Parker hadn't intended. Jessie *didn't* have time. Jasper Otis was walking free. Beto Estrada was in danger. Milly Estrada was dead in a freezer, her murder unsolved.

And there was her own life too: a new job starting up next week, a boyfriend trying to reclaim his life, and a sister just trying to keep her head above water. All that was already on the back burner at this moment and she was going to take on another responsibility?

And yet some part of her knew they'd understand. If she told them that she had a chance to stop the sex trafficking of teenage girls, but doing so required her to be here now, they'd support her. She was sure of it.

"I'll make time."

The other detective shrugged.

"Fine," she said, handing over a small piece of paper. "I looked up these files this morning. They include every mention of our mogul friend in any case in the last ten years. I also pulled all the files that allege sex crimes against an HPI."

"HPI?" Jessie repeated.

"High profile individual," Parker said. "We use the term in reports so we don't have to open the can of worms that comes from mentioning names before we're ready to charge. It protects us and allows us to do back searches without drawing attention."

"How do you distinguish among HPIs?" Jessie asked.

"We usually put a footnote in the report corresponding to the first mention of the HPI. It includes a description. You'll have to go through those footnotes to see who's under suspicion. I can tell you that our mogul friend is in there quite a bit. I believe he's described as a 'bald, middle-aged international media professional.' If you come across that phrase, you know you've got our boy."

"Okay, thanks," Jessie said. "How many files are we talking about?"

Parker looked at her with something close to pity in her eyes.

"I'd rather not say. I don't want to depress you."

*

Depressing was an understatement. Hopeless was more accurate.

After nearly two hours in the tiny annex office of the file room where she'd set up shop, Jessie needed a break. She stood and

128

stretched, trying not to let the dozens of horror stories she'd just read overwhelm her.

There were over two hundred HPI cases in the files from just the last decade. Of those, seventeen used the description that Parker told her matched Jasper Otis. In addition, there were six additional cases that specifically mentioned him by name.

But in every instance, something happened to undermine the case, making it impossible to proceed. Evidence disappeared. Victims retracted their statements around the time that their bank accounts became suddenly flush. Others were threatened with lawsuits that mentioned everything from slander to harassment. In each case, those girls retracted their statements as well. Two girls went missing soon after giving their statements. They were never found and no one followed up.

From everything that Jessie had read, Jasper Otis was a serial sexual predator. Assuming that half of what these girls claimed was true, he had committed multiple crimes. He forced bound girls to have sex with him. He ordered them to have sex with other men in front of him.

One girl alleged that he had taken a group of them on private planes to a foreign country. She and some girls returned stateside. But others were sold to men from the other country and left behind. There were other, more specific allegations that Jessie didn't feel up to replaying in her head again. Independent of whether he was responsible for Millicent Estrada's death, the man was a monster who had to be stopped.

She got a text from Hannah telling her that Nurse Patty was leaving, to be replaced by the night nurse, a guy named John. Jessie texted back that she'd be home within the hour. Then she carefully returned the files, all of which she'd taken screenshots of, to their proper locations. She didn't want to leave any out that the mole could use to retrace her steps. Then she went upstairs to confront Captain Decker with the magnitude of the situation.

She was walking across the bullpen to his office when a smallish, sweaty guy in his early twenties wearing a sweatshirt and bicycle shorts approached her. He looked so skittish that her hand involuntarily went to her holster.

"Can I help you?" she asked.

"Yes ma'am," he said politely. "I spoke to the front desk sergeant and he had me wait over in one of those chairs."

129

She looked over. He had indicated the spillover area where suspects and witnesses were held until they could be interviewed. Each chair had a metal bar across it that could attach to handcuffs if someone needed to be kept from moving about. It was rare for the general public to be allowed in the area.

"Do you have a statement to give?" she asked, confused. "Didn't someone direct you to Detective Bray?"

"No ma'am," he said, pulling something out of the backpack dangling off his shoulder.

"Careful," she warned, undoing the safety guard on the holster. "Why don't you tell me what this is about before you start yanking stuff out of bags?"

"I'm sorry, ma'am," he said. "I didn't mean to startle you. It's just an envelope with some paperwork. May I?"

"Slowly," she told him.

He delicately removed what was indeed a thick manila envelope.

"You are Jessie Hunt, correct?" he asked.

"Yeah," she answered as he handed her the envelope.

"You've been served."

CHAPTER TWENTY SIX

She read the papers in Decker's office while she waited for him to return.

The documents were from attorneys for Jasper Otis and they were endless: claims of harassment, trespassing, slander, intimidation, false imprisonment (that one was apparently related to the uneventful interrogation in his dining room), and stalking.

She couldn't help but notice how similar some of the legal allegations were to those made against the girls who claimed he'd sexually assaulted them. Though the sheer volume of allegations—twenty-two in total—was daunting, they weren't having the effect she suspected was intended.

Rather than feeling intimidated, she was just pissed. Jasper Otis didn't seem to understand that he was using his power to bully someone who had literally faced down death multiple times. She didn't know how this would play out, but Jessie wasn't going to back down. If Otis had done his research, he would have known better.

That's when Decker walked in.

"What's wrong?" he asked, immediately sensing something was amiss.

"Look at this," she told him, handing over the lawsuit.

She watched as he read it. His face turned into a frown that grew increasingly severe. But as he finished the last page, he broke into a wry grin.

"I consider it a good thing," he said, handing it back to her.

She was stunned at his reaction.

"I'd love to hear how you came to that conclusion," she said.

He started to speak, then stopped himself.

"Care to join me for a walk?" he asked.

She nodded. Neither of them spoke until they were in the courtyard.

"This means you've got them rattled," he said when they got to a secluded section. "They don't file twenty-two-allegation lawsuits against someone they're not worried about."

Jessie appreciated the sentiment but didn't want him to forget about the practical concerns.

"They may be worried," she said. "But I'm the one who's going to have the huge legal bill."

Decker shook his head paternally.

"Don't worry about that," he said. "The consulting contract you signed for this case protects you. The department will foot any legal fees you incur during the course of your investigation. The higher-ups may be scared of Otis but they also know that if they cave on this, it will be open season for harassment lawsuits against cops doing basic police work."

"But I'm not a cop," she reminded him.

"This is the rare occasion in which you actually have the best of both worlds. You're a private citizen not bound by every department rule. But you have the legal resources of the LAPD at your disposal. I suspect the consultant policy may be revised if this lawsuit bankrupts the department. But that's a concern for another day."

Jessie allowed herself to be heartened by what he said, even if some small part of her feared the department would cut her loose if things got too messy. Instead of obsessing over that, she moved on.

"Any luck overturning the stay for our search warrant at the Otis Estate?" she asked.

He responded with a wry chuckle.

"Still working on it," he said. "I think it may happen, but not today. The key is, once it's overturned, you have to be ready to execute the warrant immediately. I suspect Otis will find another judge to reverse it again ASAP, which means you'll only have a brief window to get in there and look around. Make sure all your ducks are in a row."

"Detective Bray's been working on it," she assured him. "She says we can have units on site within ten minutes of any ruling, day or night."

"Good," he said. "What else have you got for me?"

She walked him through what she'd learned from the cold case files that Detective Parker had flagged for her. With each revelation, the creases in his forehead seemed to get deeper.

"Obviously, don't tell anyone about this," he said when she was done. "Not Detective Bray, not your young researcher friend, no one. I've created a secure cloud account for just the two of us. Send a copy of the files there. Otherwise, don't distribute them anywhere. We'll share them when the time is right."

Jessie nodded.

"I'm assuming all these precautions mean you're no closer to uncovering the mole who stole the thumb drive from Parker's locker?"

"I don't have anything official on that," he said cryptically. "But I wouldn't say 'no closer.' There's movement."

"Well, whoever did it is definitely not a free agent," she said, telling him about her visit to Beto Estrada without naming names.

He listened intently as if what she was saying comported with suspicions he already had but wouldn't share. When he replied, it was more generally.

"Once the mole is caught, we can make our next move."

"What would that be?" Jessie asked.

"Get someone to go on the record—maybe the mole, maybe someone from one of these cases who hasn't settled, maybe a new victim, maybe the source who gave you the file. Once someone speaks out, the floodgates should open."

"You think someone will really speak out against Jasper Otis?" Jessie asked skeptically, "Because I'm pretty sure my source won't."

"We'll see," he said with more confidence than she would have expected. "I have some tools at my disposal that I prefer not to share just now. I may be old, Hunt, but I'm also wily."

"But—" she started to say.

"No more 'buts' tonight. It's getting late. Don't you have folks waiting for you at home?"

Jessie looked at her watch. It was already 5:36 and she'd promised Hannah she'd be home for dinner at six. A rush of angst passed through her as she realized she was in danger of violating her promise.

"Yes," she said. "If I'm not home in twenty-four minutes, I may have to sleep in the backyard hammock."

She was already halfway across the courtyard when she heard Decker call out "good luck."

*

Jessie made it with three minutes to spare.

After dinner, John the night nurse helped Hannah with the dishes. Jessie retreated to the guest bedroom to change. Suddenly the weight of the day hit her. She had a source afraid he was a dead man walking. She'd uncovered a massive sex-trafficking ring that had been essentially ignored for a decade. She kept hitting dead ends in her murder investigation. A billionaire mixed up in both was suing her into the ground. Her wheelchair-bound, barely verbal boyfriend looked completely wiped out from his first full day at home. And, though Hannah was all smiles, Jessie got the unsettling feeling that her half-sister was hiding something big. Her thoughts were interrupted by a knock on the door.

"It's open," she said.

Hannah opened it, a look of trepidation on her face.

"Can I talk to you about something?" she asked.

"Of course. Come on in."

Hannah entered and closed the door behind her, a sure sign that this wasn't going to be a chat about her calculus grade.

"I have to tell you something," she said. "When you hear it, you might be a little pissed at me. But you have to promise not to interrupt or say anything until I'm done."

"Okay."

"I need you to promise," Hannah reiterated.

"I promise," Jessie said, wanting to give the girl space to be honest but terrified at what she might be about to hear.

Hannah proceeded to walk her through the events culminating in this afternoon's drive with Rico. She mentioned the first approach from Elodie weeks ago; how it seemed to fit with Jessie's suspicion about a sex ring; that she'd engaged Elodie today; the ride she'd taken with Rico; what he'd revealed and what he expected of her tomorrow.

"I recorded the whole conversation with him," she concluded. "I got his license plate number. I couldn't risk taking his picture without him noticing but I was able to sneak one of Elodie. I have all of it on my phone."

She seemed to be done. Jessie waited an extra moment to be sure before speaking.

"Are you okay?" she finally asked.

"I had a little moment after it was over," Hannah admitted. "Kind of a delayed freak-out where I realized it could have gone bad and you might have found my head in a dumpster. But yeah, I'm okay. You think this stuff will help with the case?"

Jessie looked at her little sister and took a deep breath, trying to give the impression that she was evaluating the value of the information, which she couldn't accurately assess yet. Hannah had an expectant expression her face, as if she was waiting to be thanked for her contribution to the investigation.

134

This was a delicate moment. Her little sister had put herself in real danger—danger that still existed—without seeming to have any real sense of what she'd gotten herself into. She appeared more excited by the intrigue of the situation than concerned for her own safety.

And yet, she'd been trying to help. Jessie had spent so much time worrying that Hannah might be conscienceless. Discovering now she had put herself at risk in the hopes of helping other young women was strangely heartening. She didn't want to quash that instinct. Moreover, she'd been honest about it when she knew that it could get her into trouble. Jessie wanted to reinforce that impulse, not undermine it.

"Thank you for telling me," she began delicately. "I'll definitely take all the information you got and see if it can be useful. I really appreciate that you were trying to make a difference."

"But you're pissed," Hannah said, her hopeful expression starting to turn sour.

"No," Jessie said quickly. "I'm not pissed. I'm concerned, for the very reasons you mentioned. This Rico guy is expecting you to go with him to meet his boss tomorrow. That obviously can't happen. They may have already done a background check on you based on your name. You're no longer safe. That's what I'm focused on—making sure that nothing bad happens to you. I was just hoping we could make it to the end of the year without any kind of threat to your life."

"Wishful thinking," Hannah muttered.

"Probably, but a girl can dream. So we're going to do what we need to do to keep you safe. I'll reach out to the right folks to follow up on this. If it's connected to the trafficking ring I mentioned, we'll pursue that. Even if it's not, we'll roll these people up and take some bad actors off the street. You'll be responsible for making that happen. You should feel proud about that. I just wish you would have discussed it with me beforehand."

"In a million years, you would never have let me get in that car," Hannah insisted. "And I never would have gotten the recording."

"You're probably right," Jessie admitted. "But can you blame me?"

They left it there. As soon as Hannah stepped out of the room, Jessie texted Gaylene Parker.

"Need to talk in person first thing tomorrow."

Within seconds, she got a thumbs-up emoji. With that done, she helped Ryan settle in for bed. He'd been quiet all evening, which she'd attributed to his exhaustion. But once they were in his bedroom alone together, he motioned for her to sit beside him on the bed.

"What's wrong?" he asked slowly.

She smiled. Even in his exhausted state, with her doing her best to hide her struggles, she couldn't fool him.

"Just having a rough workday," she said. "You know how it is. Sometimes everything seems to come in waves. It's just a real storm right now."

"Otis?" he asked.

She stared at him, amazed.

"How did you know that?" she asked.

"Watch news," he huffed. "Hear you on the phone. Ears still work."

She worried he was upset that she'd underestimated him, but he was smiling as he said it.

"I forgot," she admitted. "You just can't shut off that detective brain, can you?"

"Never," he said with more vigor in his voice than she'd heard from him since the injury.

"I don't want to bore you with the details, especially before bed," she told him as she grabbed his hand and squeezed. "Let's just say that solving a murder connected to a vindictive, amoral billionaire who may be involved in a criminal conspiracy that I can't talk about definitely makes for a tiring day."

He squeezed her hand back.

"Look...at me," he said firmly.

She did. He continued, clearly, and without pausing for breath.

"No one better at this than you. No one better to bring this guy down. Stay strong. Love you."

Only after he said it did he sink back against his pillow, worn out by the effort of what he'd needed to convey.

"Thanks, babe," she said, wiping tears away with her free hand. "You don't know how badly I needed to hear that."

But his smile told her that he did know. And he was right. She could do this. And she would.

CHAPTER TWENTY SEVEN

Jessie only slept until 4:30. There was a lot to do this morning. Her first call was to Decker.

"A team is ready to execute a search warrant on Otis's house the second the stay is lifted," he told her.

"Excellent," she replied. "By the way, Hannah's going to need undercover cops watching her at school today for reasons I'll explain when we talk in person."

"Speaking of in-person conversations, check in with Jamil when you get to the station. He has some updates for you."

When Nurse Patty came to relieve Nurse John, Jessie and Hannah left too. Ryan was still asleep so Jessie asked Patty to call when he woke up so she could say good morning.

"Our plan for your school day is being revised," she told Hannah when they were in the car. "We'll be making a pit stop at the police station first. I'll explain everything soon."

Once they arrived at the station, everything happened in quick succession. She pulled up in front.

"We're here," she texted Decker.

A minute later he and Detective Parker emerged and hopped in the back seat of the car. Jessie made the two-minute drive to Nickel Diner, where she'd had so many heart to heart conversations with Garland Moses. But this visit would be different.

When they walked in a server ushered them to the secluded banquette in the back corner, one that Decker had called to reserve. All three law enforcement professionals were equally paranoid that the police station wasn't safe for extremely sensitive conversations. And after their multiple chats in the courtyard, Jessie noted that she was worried that someone might have even placed a listening device out there. The hope was that moving quickly and unexpectedly, they could stay ahead of prying ears.

"Give it to us quick. I don't know how long we have," Decker said as soon as they sat down. He pulled out a small box and placed it on the table. "This is a high frequency blocking device. It should offer some temporary protection."

Jessie dived in, giving the basics of Hannah's story while simultaneously sending Decker and Parker the audio recording, license plate, and photo of Elodie Peters. She mentioned the planned meeting with Rico's boss this afternoon. Parker, her head down, furiously took notes the whole time. When Jessie finished, the detective spoke quickly.

"Here's what I recommend. Based on your request to the captain earlier, we already have two undercover officers lined up for the day, one male and one female. They're both experienced in high school environments. We're already coordinating with the school for at least one of them to be in each of Hannah's classes throughout the day. The other will tail Elodie."

"Won't that seem suspicious to her?" Hannah asked. "Two new kids showing up in her classes?"

"Unlikely," Parker said. "We'll rotate them. They won't interact with her more than necessary. There's no reason she would make any connection. Hannah—after school you will ride with one officer to the corner where Rico expects to meet you and identify him in his vehicle. That will be the extent of your involvement."

Jessie was relieved to hear that, even as she saw that Hannah was disappointed.

"Wouldn't it be better for me to play along so that he takes me to meet his boss?" she asked.

"It's too risky," Parker said. "The minute you get in his car, hell, the minute he sees you, you're in jeopardy. As Jessie said, they may have already looked into your background. If they have, they might have figured out that your story doesn't add up. We don't know how Rico will react. We don't know if he'll have people with him. There are just too many variables. Instead, one officer will escort you home while the other follows Rico in conjunction with other unmarked units. We may ask you to text Elodie to have her tell Rico you're not feeling well and need to postpone."

"Why?" Hannah asked.

"We'll need some excuse for you not to show up, no matter how lame," Parker explained. "We don't want Rico to get spooked. We still want him to go to his boss's place this afternoon."

Hannah seemed unhappy with the plan but Parker, unmoved, fixed her steady gaze on the girl.

"Your job, other than to text Elodie that you're cancelling the meet, is to have a normal day. Go to your classes. Do your work. If Elodie approaches you, act as if everything is still on for this afternoon. Don't try to record her or get additional information. We don't want to spook her either and have her warn Rico off. Is that all clear?"

Hannah nodded that it was. Parker continued.

"Great. We're going to take a few extra precautions when we leave here. The captain and I are going to head out now and walk back to the station. You two will leave a couple of minutes later. Your sister will drop you off at the Pershing metro station," she said to Hannah as she held up her phone. "This woman, who is one of the undercover officers you'll be with at school all day, is currently sitting on a bench outside the station entrance. Her name's Marie. She'll follow you down the escalator. At the bottom, she'll pass you. Follow her without making contact. She'll lead you to a separate exit, where you'll both be met by a car. Once you get in, she'll explain the details from there."

When she was done, Decker turned to Jessie.

"When you get back to the station, find me and we'll deal with the other pending matters."

With that, the captain and Parker got up and left. Jessie and Hannah waited two minutes before doing the same. As they walked out, it occurred to Jessie that after seating them, no one from the diner had approached them, even to offer coffee. Apparently Captain Decker had trained the staff here well.

A few minutes later, they pulled up at the station entrance. Marie, the undercover cop, was scrolling disinterestedly through her phone. Jessie was amazed at how young the girl looked in person. She had to be in her early twenties but with her floral dress, sneakers, and high ponytail, she could easily pass for sixteen.

"Remember, don't acknowledge her in any way, just in case you're being watched," Jessie said. "I'll be in touch throughout the day with any relevant updates. Please stay safe."

"I will, Mom," Hannah said playfully, dramatically rolling her eyes.

Jessie knew her sister was attempting to puncture the intensity of the situation and decided it was best to just play along.

"In that case, have a nice day, dear," she said, adopting her best June Cleaver tone.

Hannah got out and walked to the escalator, impressively not even glancing in the cop's direction. For a few seconds, the officer didn't move, making Jessie worry that she truly hadn't seen Hannah. But then she casually got up, never taking her eyes off her phone screen, and ambled toward the escalator. Only when she disappeared from sight did Jessie finally, reluctantly pull out.

CHAPTER TWENTY EIGHT

Decker was waiting anxiously when Jessie got back.

When she stepped into the bullpen, he was wandering among different units, ostensibly checking in with all the detective teams. But she could tell he was antsy. When she caught his eye, he motioned for her to follow him out to the courtyard. Despite her apprehension that it might not be secure, she did. But just as he was about to open the exterior door, he suddenly changed directions and headed for a maintenance closet a little ways down the hall. He stepped in and she followed a few moments later.

"I'll be brief," he whispered, locking the door after her. "First, I just got word that the stay will be lifted at one p.m. I'll receive a copy of the order at one oh-one and send it to you and Bray immediately. You should probably be outside the Otis Estate gate waiting."

"We will be," Jessie assured him.

Despite her best efforts to stay cool and collected, she felt a surge of excitement course through her. It was finally happening.

"As to our other concern about leaks, I've got good and bad news," Decker continued. "As I feared, all the footage from the time Parker's secure locker was infiltrated was wiped clean. A generic access card, untraceable to any particular individual, was used to gain admittance to different areas."

"I'm hoping that's the bad news," Jessie said.

"It is. Like I said yesterday, I'm old but wily. Without getting into specifics, I'll just say that, based on certain patterns associated with how and when access was gained, I've been able to narrow down the list of likely culprits. And your well-placed concern that the courtyard might no longer be secure either may help me narrow it even further. I hope to know more later today."

"That's it?" Jessie said. "You can't tell me who I should be watching out for?"

"I genuinely don't know yet. And I wouldn't want to tip that person off if I did know. We could turn a liability into an asset if we play this right. But for that to happen, you have to stay focused on your case.

Find out what happened to Millicent Estrada. Hopefully the other stuff will fall into place."

"Speaking of," Jessie noted, "I've gotten multiple texts from both Detective Bray and Jamil in the last few minutes. I think they're anxious to discuss developments. I should probably go see what's up."

Decker's only response was to unlock the door and hold it open for her. She hurried out, headed toward Research. She was almost there when she stopped in her tracks. Something Decker had said moments earlier was bouncing around in her brain, making it itch in that way she knew she shouldn't ignore.

He had told her to find out what happened to Millicent Estrada. And while she knew what he had meant—that she should find out who murdered the woman—it occurred to her that she should be focusing on the larger question: *what happened* to Milly.

Jessie had been so busy running around, trying to get stays lifted, studying surveillance footage, and listening to audio files from trafficked young girls that she'd lost sight of her purpose. To find out what happened to Milly, she had to understand *why it happened*, and that meant profiling the killer, not the victim.

Instead of going to Research, Jessie stepped out into the courtyard. There was still a chill in the morning air, which she found clarifying. She sat on a shaded bench and closed her eyes, allowing her breathing to slow and her mind to clear.

After a minute, she let her brain relax and go wherever it chose. The first image that popped into her mind was of Milly's blouse, lying on the floor beside Jasper Otis's bed.

However it had ended up there, the fact that the buttons had been undone, rather than ripped off, suggested that, despite how Milly had been found—half naked in a shower—this hadn't started as an assault. Either that blouse had been removed voluntarily or it had been removed after her death, without any resistance.

There was bruising on Milly's body. But the medical examiner said there were no scratches on her, meaning the perpetrator had likely gotten close to her without a fight. That implied it was someone she knew and was comfortable with.

It was possible that the encounter had begun consensually before turning violent. She'd explored that theory a bit. But another theory, one she'd mentioned to Decker in passing but never truly considered, was that the incident wasn't about sex at all. What if it was just made to look that way afterward to throw investigators off? What if Milly had been killed for another reason entirely?

If that was the case and this wasn't a moment of passion gone awry, it meant that whoever had killed her wasn't worried about time. People in a panicky rush don't methodically undo all the buttons on someone's shirt.

And if the killer wasn't worried about time, that meant it was someone who wasn't afraid they'd be discovered in the residential wing, or even in Otis's personal space. It was someone who felt like they belonged there. Add that to the possibility that Milly knew her attacker and suddenly the pool of likely killers got pretty small. There were only a few people at the estate that night who both knew Milly *and* had free rein of the residential wing.

Clearly Jasper Otis was one of them. He had dozens of alibi witnesses, not even including his unnamed lady friend, though Jessie was skeptical of all of them. On the other hand, Davey Pasternak had zero witnesses but didn't seem like the type to have the run of the Otis Estate. But there were others.

Jessie got up from the bench and rushed to the Research department to see if Jamil could rule any of them in or out. When she walked in, she got exasperated looks from both him and Karen, who were hunched over the same monitor.

"Glad you could join us," Karen said, trying to sound jokey but failing to hide her frustration.

"Sorry, guys," Jessie said. "I'm currently juggling five balls with two hands. I understand you've got some updates."

"Quite a few," Jamil said, returning his gaze to the screen. "You're not going to like any of them."

"Way to sell it, Jamil," she replied.

"Sorry," he said. "I figured I'd just rip the Band-Aid off."

"Rip away," she said, waving her hand as she took a seat beside him.

"Okay, let's deal with Nancy Salter first. I noticed that after she cold-cocked that caterer, she texted someone. It got me thinking. Even though I couldn't track her location using her phone, maybe I could track it using her texts. Turns out I could, kind of."

Jessie waited for him to continue but he seemed hesitant, as if she might shoot him down.

"Go ahead," she said. "Your job is to give me the facts, whether I like them or not."

143

That seemed to set him at ease a bit.

"Right, so I found the corresponding text from after the caterer incident, at five forty-six a.m. She told one of her staffers that she wanted to look into a new catering company because the current one was incompetent. So we know the text matches her expected location. She sent multiple other texts throughout the night, all very demanding, most unpleasant. I won't depress you with the details. But there were two in particular I wanted to draw your attention to."

He punched up a new screen that included the texts with their timestamp and what appeared to be locations on the estate.

"So," he continued, "other than these two texts it's basically impossible to verify Salter's location at the time they were sent. Despite their vitriol, they either weren't specific enough or nowhere near a camera. But these are different."

He enlarged one text. It read: *Buster's wreaking havoc. Getting complaints. Don't need a lawsuit. Kick him out.* The timestamp was 2:57 a.m.

"Now look," he said.

He played a video time stamped 3:04 a.m. from the South House main entrance. It showed the door open and a portly, balding man being escorted forcefully to an area to the west of the roundabout, where several taxis were waiting. He was placed in one, which pulled out seconds later.

"What did I just see?" Jessie asked.

"That was Buster Catalano, the comedian."

"The guy who does impressions of people no one cares about," Karen added.

"Right," Jamil said. "He's also notorious for being grabby. He's been sued for sexual harassment twice. It appears that he was up to his old tricks and Salter wasn't happy about it. In fact, she was so unhappy that she personally supervised his removal from the estate."

He recentered the image and magnified it to show a figure standing in the doorway, watching Buster being taken away. The face was cut off because of the camera angle but the business suit and doily scarf were visible. Jamil looked over at Jessie proudly.

"We couldn't mark her location with facial recognition earlier because there was no face to recognize."

"That's good, Jamil," she said, "really good. What's the other text?"

144

Jamil pulled that one up. It read: *Be there in 2 min.* It was from 3:13 a.m.

"So I checked to see what she was replying to," Jamil said. "And it was this."

He pulled up a text from someone named Mary Proul. It read: *Grease fire extinguished in the kitchen. Ugly mess. Smoky. Please advise.*

"This is what we see a few minutes after that," he said, zooming in on a small open space between the junctions of the South House and East House. "According to the house plans, that's the side door of the service kitchen."

At 3:22 a.m., a young woman walked out the open door, disappeared briefly from the frame, and returned with a wheeled trash bin. Someone who couldn't quite be seen tossed several bags of trash in the bin. Jamil froze the frame, then pulled cropped images of the person's sleeves and shoes over to another monitor. He then pulled images of the sleeves and shoes Nancy Salter wore at the main entrance when Buster Catalano was kicked out. They matched exactly.

"So that's her then?" Jessie said, verbalizing the obvious.

"It would seem so. She drops in additional trash bags at three twenty-six and three thirty-two."

"Okay, Jamil," Jessie said. "Why don't you pull up the timeline I know you've created and are dying to show me?"

Jamil smiled at her, then pushed a button. A timeline appeared on the screen. It was titled "Millicent Estrada window of death" and read: 3:00 to 3:50 a.m. He hit another button and a new timeline appeared below the first. It was titled "Nancy Salter time accounted for." It read: 2:57 a.m. to 3:06 a.m. and 3:13 a.m.to 3:32 a.m.

"So," Jessie concluded, "while it was technically possible for Nancy Salter to have killed Milly, she would have had an extremely tight window and she would have had to go from the far end of one wing of the estate to the opposite end of another wing. Is that what you're telling me?"

"That's what I'm telling you," Jamil confirmed.

Jessie sighed. Her suspicion of Salter wasn't completely disproven but it was looking like one of her most promising suspects almost certainly had to be removed from the list.

"Okay," she said. "What other bad news have you got for me?"

"I actually have one bit of good news I can toss in to shake things up."

145

"Please," Jessie replied. "I'll take what I can get."

"You asked me to check on the security footage from Beto Estrada's house and let you know if I found anything unusual. I did. All the cameras cut out from nine fourteen a.m. to ten twenty-two a.m. For over an hour, it was just static. Then they magically turned on again."

He was looking at her hopefully, as if he might have brightened her day with news that actually confirmed her concerns about Estrada's house being tapped. She didn't have the heart to burst his bubble.

"Great job, Jamil," she told him reassuringly. "Now you can go back to the bad news."

Jamil looked over cautiously at Karen, who shrugged.

"Just tell her," she said. "Remember, we're in Band-Aid ripping mode here."

Jamil still seemed wary, but gulped and went for it anyway.

"You know those other big names you wanted me to check into, the senator, the actor, and the sultan?"

"Yeah," Jessie replied.

"It looks like you may have to cross them off the list too."

"Why is that?"

"Senator Johnson was in Washington, D.C., last weekend. Paul Gilliard is shooting a movie on location in Santa Fe, New Mexico. And the sultan, whose full name is Omar Abdul Salah and appears to be worth over a billion dollars based on my research, was on a flight home from Paris on Saturday."

Jessie nodded quietly. Jamil was exploding every potential option in her tiny bucket of remaining suspects. As she sat swiveling in the chair in the darkened research room, she allowed the complete failure of their investigation to settle in.

Almost all of their suspects had airtight alibis. Even Jasper Otis, who Jessie still liked for this, had multiple witnesses who'd offered statements on his behalf. Without formal evidence to contradict their claims, he would skate, just like he'd skated on all the sexual allegations made against him. It was infuriating to know that her most credible suspect kept slipping just out of her grasp.

The only person without a solid alibi was the Humbert Humbert roadie, Davey Pasternak. Jessie was actually surprised that Karen hadn't already suggested they leave to pick him up. She guessed that it was just a polite delay, so as not to rub salt in the wound.

She closed her eyes as she swiveled. Something was still eating at her, something she couldn't quite put her finger on. It was poking at her, teasing her, taunting her. It came down to this: She couldn't get past the idea that Milly's killer felt comfortable enough to carefully remove her blouse, then place her in a shower and turn on the water.

Who other than Otis would feel comfortable in the residential wing, as if they owned the place? And who knew Milly Estrada well enough that she'd let down her guard? Jessie opened her eyes.

"Do we have visual evidence of all three of those men being elsewhere or is that just what their schedules say?" she asked.

Jamil looked taken aback, then slightly embarrassed.

"Just schedules," he admitted. "After I found those, I stopped looking."

"That's okay," Jessie told him, not wanting to be too harsh. "But we should look now."

"What are you thinking?" Karen asked.

Jessie smiled at her even though she had no credible reason to.

"I'd be willing to bet that we won't find a single photo of one of them in the location his schedule says he was supposed to be."

"Why not?" Karen asked.

"Because I think Milly's killer is still in that house."

CHAPTER TWENTY NINE

Jessie's eyes were blurry from studying screens so intently.

They'd spent the last half hour reviewing alibis and she decided it was time for everyone to give an update on the suspect they'd been looking into. Karen was investigating Paul Hilliard because she had the most insight into the Hollywood community. Jamil was following up Sultan Salah because it involved technical understanding of flight patterns and airport footage. That left Jessie with Senator Johnson, who had the most public schedule. She started first.

"I think we can officially rule the senator out," she said. "He didn't have any formal events over the weekend. But an 'on the town' item for the *Post* mentions a brunch sighting of him on Saturday afternoon in D.C., and he posted footage of himself from his kid's soccer game on Sunday afternoon, also in D.C. That doesn't leave him much time to fly to L.A. for an all-night party and still get back."

"The sultan may be a dead end too," Jamil told them. "I found security footage of him in a Paris jewelry store on Saturday three hours before he was scheduled to fly home. I also pulled video from the airport where he landed. It's grainy but facial recognition has the guy exiting the plane as a seventy-four-percent match to Sultan Salah."

"So that just leaves our Oscar winner," Jessie said. "What did you find, Karen?"

"It's a little weird, actually," the detective said.

Jessie perked up. Weird was better than nothing.

"Weird how?" she asked.

"First of all, Gilliard has been on location in Santa Fe for the last month shooting a western. But I checked the production bulletin. According to the call sheets, his last shooting day was Friday. I called the production office and they said they're in the middle of shooting an extended gunfight. He's not a part of it so he's off until tomorrow."

"Did they say where he was?" Jessie asked.

"Nope. As long as he shows up on set when he's needed, they don't keep tabs on him."

"So he could have come back to L.A.?" Jessie pressed.

"Possibly," Karen said. "Unfortunately, it will take a while to check flight manifests to see if his name comes up."

"There might be another way," Jamil said, pulling up a new screen.

"What's that?" Jessie asked.

"On the right is the archived footage from the South House main entrance," he said, pointing. "On the left is the live feed of the entrance right now."

"How do you have the live video feed from a place we can't even get a search warrant for?" Jessie asked, astounded.

Jamil smiled gleefully. Jessie could tell that these were the moments he lived for.

"Before they shut down all cooperation, I spoke to a helpful security guy there. He's actually interested in joining the department. Anyway, he gave me all their available archived video for the last week. He also let me patch into their live feed. I think he was trying to impress me. But apparently that didn't get conveyed to his bosses because the feed is still active. I don't think they'd allow it if they knew we had access."

"How does that help us?" Karen asked.

Jamil looked like he wanted to enjoy this moment a little longer but seemed to sense it wouldn't be appreciated.

"We've only done facial recognition from Saturday evening to Sunday midday because we assumed that the murderer arrived for the party and left when it ended. But with the archived footage, we can check to see if Gilliard arrived earlier and left later."

His fingers flew over the keyboard for a few seconds before he looked up again.

"Done," he said. "We should have the results soon."

Jessie didn't want to waste any time.

"I need to make a quick call," she said. "Keep me posted."

She walked out to her car, turned on the radio, and made the call. When it picked up, she spoke quietly.

"Are you at work?" she asked and when she learned the answer was yes continued. "I need your help."

*

When Jessie dashed back into the research room fifteen minutes later, she was so short of breath she couldn't speak at first.

"Are you okay?" Karen asked, worried.

149

"I've got news," Jessie panted. "But I can't say where I got it."

Both of them stared at her, waiting. She held up her hand while she sucked in air.

I really need to get in better shape.

When she was finally able to speak normally again, she launched in.

"Milly Estrada was Gilliard's lawyer," she said. "It didn't show up in the files we looked at when we were at her office on Sunday because they limited our access exclusively to clients who had cases before a court and he never did. But she's represented him for years. My source wouldn't get more specific than that. But they did share that her phone logs from work show that she had multiple conversations with Gilliard this week, including a call on Friday afternoon."

Jamil immediately pulled up a new window and began a search. Within seconds, he had several tabs open and began flipping among them.

"It looks like he hasn't posted on any social media outlet since Thursday night," he said. "Kind of odd, considering that up until then, he was active on all of them."

A beep from one of the monitors made them all turn in that direction.

"What's that about?" Karen asked.

"The facial recognition search just ended," Jamil said. "And look what we have here. Paul Gilliard arrived at the Otis Estate at four forty-one on Friday afternoon. And at least according to the footage we have, it looks like he never left."

He turned back to Jessie with a gleam in his eye.

"What now?" he asked.

"Now," Jessie told them both, "I think it's time we got to know Mr. Gilliard a little better."

CHAPTER THIRTY

Jasper Otis was having a rough week, and almost all of it had to do with the Estradas.

As he walked down the hall from his business office in East House back to the residence in West House, he did a mental check-in to review where he stood. He had ongoing challenges with Beto, which would hopefully be definitively resolved soon. But the problems stemming from Beto's ex-wife, Milly, were more immediately pressing.

What had begun as helping out an old friend had gotten unexpectedly messy. He had known from the first second there was a problem, when his cell phone rang at 3:30 a.m. and the caller ID said it came from his own bedroom. When he picked up, he heard Paul Gilliard's desperate voice on the line.

"I screwed up, buddy," Paul said. "And I need your help."

"What is it?"

"I was with Milly Estrada, you know the lawyer? We were getting hot and heavy in your room and I took a little something to amp everything up and it got out of control. I got too excited, I guess, and I accidentally…yanked her neck too hard and it broke. She's dead, Jasper."

"What?" Jasper had asked, not sure he'd heard it right.

"I guess I don't know my own strength and with everything I'm on right now, I didn't even realize what I'd done."

Jasper remembered trying to process the information as he lay next to the barely legal model he'd spent most of the last hour with, the one whose name he didn't want to tell the cops because she had only officially turned eighteen hours earlier. Suddenly his raucous bacchanal had turned into a potentially empire-destroying nightmare. He remembered getting up and going into the bathroom where he could whisper without being heard.

"Just turn yourself in, Paul," he'd insisted. "I'll get you the best lawyers. We'll show that it was the drugs that did this, not you."

"You don't get it," Paul pleaded. "Milly *was* the best lawyer. She's the one who saved me when I got in trouble before. If I turn myself in, all of that will come out. I'll spend the rest of my life in prison."

Jasper, who was feeling the effects of some chemicals he'd ingested over the course of the night, felt panic rise in his chest.

"They're going to find out it was you, Paul. They'll check for DNA or something. Better to go on offense and massage the story as best you can."

"No," Paul said emphatically. "We never actually did anything so there's nothing to trace. Besides, I put her in your shower with the water running. Any physical evidence will be washed away. By the time she's found, there will be nothing to collect. And if you have your maids clean up the place as soon as she's discovered, then that will compromise the crime scene."

"How am I supposed to justify doing that when the cops come?" Jasper hissed.

"I don't know. Just say you couldn't have a dead body in your bathroom—that it was too much for you. The police around here aren't going to push you, of all people, too hard."

"It's too risky," Jasper persisted.

There was a long silence on the other end of the line. Somehow, he knew what was coming.

"You know what was risky?" Paul said coldly. "Putting my career on the line for you. Do I have to remind you about that party where I found you with that girl? Do you remember how I convinced her mom not to go to the cops by giving her a producer credit on my movie? Do you remem—?"

"Okay, okay. I get it," Jasper said. "You don't have to go there. We'll get this done."

But now, three days later, it still wasn't done. He was barely holding off the cops. Paul was still holed up in his home. And the possibility that his own proclivities might come to light was still frighteningly real.

He had to convince Paul that it was time to go. Oscar-winning matinee idols didn't just drop off the grid for days on end anymore. He was going to be missed soon. And if he was still at Otis Estate when questions started getting asked, the consequences would be bad for everyone, especially him.

So instead of going back to his wing to ponder, he went to see Paul.

152

Jessie had never been a Paul Gilliard fan.

Of course she'd seen some of his movies. He was one of the biggest movie stars in the world. She knew she was in the minority, but she always thought he projected a slightly smarmy vibe that was reinforced by his over-tanned skin, over-sculpted hair, and over-ripped muscles.

But she'd never had cause to think of him beyond that surface level. Now that she was diving deeper, she discovered that her instincts had been right on. The guy had never formally been charged with any crimes but he'd come close several times.

"When I worked West L.A. division," Karen said, "I heard multiple stories from patrol officers about neighbors calling, concerned about screaming fights coming from his place. They never found any obvious evidence of violence when they did welfare checks, and none of his girlfriends ever filed complaints. But I was told that sometimes they looked scared. It was never enough to act on. And it was so long ago that I forgot about it until now."

Jessie had been studying a suspicious file of her own.

"Not enough to go on seems to be a pattern," she said. "Do you know about his wife?"

"I thought that was an accident," Karen said.

"What was?" asked Jamil, who'd been focused on his own task. "I think that was before my time."

Karen filled him in.

"Seven years ago, he and his wife were skiing. The ski lift safety bar was defective and she fell out of the chair, hundreds of feet to the ground. She died on impact. Gilliard almost fell too. They found him clinging to the chair. At least that was the official story."

"Right," Jessie confirmed. "Conveniently, that was exactly the time that Millicent Estrada became his primary criminal lawyer. According to everything I've found, she pushed hard for the case to be closed quickly. It was ruled an accident. He was never formally investigated. Gilliard even filed suit against the ski lodge, though Milly didn't represent him on that case. But he eventually dropped it, saying going to court would be too painful."

"That's convenient," Jamil noted. "If it had gone to trial, there would have been all kinds of discovery that might have revealed new evidence."

"So he got to look like the angry widower, fighting for justice for his wife," Karen said, "before becoming the widower too grief-stricken to pursue it. I remember the whole country mourned for him. But why does that matter now?"

Jessie smiled. This was what she'd been waiting for.

"Maybe because the two of them hadn't seen each other in years," she said. "According to my source, Milly had only bumped into Gilliard in the last few months, once she started getting back on the social circuit after her divorce."

"Why is that significant?" Jamil asked.

This was usually the moment where Jessie got chastised by Ryan for letting her intuition trump the evidence at hand. But he wasn't here and she got the sense that her audience was ready to take the ride with her, so she launched in.

"I have a theory. What if Paul Gilliard killed his wife? What if he pushed her off that lift, maybe in a moment of anger, maybe for some other reason? What if Milly Estrada knew that and helped him cover it up, shut down the investigation? She wasn't as established back then. Getting him as a client was major coup. What if she let her ambition trump her ethics? The whole mess is taken care of and she doesn't have to think about it for years afterward. She's still his criminal lawyer but he keeps his nose clean so she is able to move on with her life."

"But that changed," Karen suggested.

"Exactly," Jessie said. "A few months ago, she gets divorced, starts going to parties, traveling in the same circles as Gilliard. She can't avoid him. And she can't avoid the memory of what she did—whatever that may have been—to help him escape justice. She starts to feel guilty. And then, according to her phone logs, she has several calls with him last week. What if she was feeling guilty enough that she was considering coming clean? What if she was trying to convince Gilliard to do the same? Maybe he agrees to confess and says he wants to come up with a plan, but not in the office, where he says his presence would be noted. He wants to do it somewhere where no one would notice them having a conversation; no one would draw any conclusions, because of the sheer number of people there. So he says he'll be at the Otis party this Saturday and asks her to come there to discuss it."

"You think he lured her there to kill her?" Karen asked.

"Maybe he genuinely wanted to change her mind and got angry when she wouldn't," Jessie said. "Maybe he planned it all along. Either way, it's murder."

Both Karen and Jamil sat quietly for a moment, pondering the hypothesis. Jessie took it as a good sign that neither had dismissed it out of hand. Finally Karen raised a question.

"But why would Jasper Otis cover for him?" she asked. "There's no way Gilliard could have covered this up and stayed at the estate this long without Otis's knowledge and consent. Why would he put himself on the line for the guy?"

"That's a good question," Jessie conceded. "Maybe Otis didn't want the bad press and acted rashly. Maybe he was just trying to be a good friend. Maybe Gilliard had something on him."

She had an idea what that might be but decided to hold off on voicing that suspicion for now. Before she could expound any further, Jamil waved his hand to get their attention.

"Got something?" Jessie asked.

"Yep," he said. "I did the search you mentioned about mold remediation. Anything like what you said they claimed was going on in the residential wing requires a clearance inspection before work can be done. The approved clearance has to be filed with the city. No such approval was filed for Otis Estate at any point in the last month."

"Well, that's suspicious," Karen said.

"Also, Nancy Salter told you the remediation process was underway, correct?" Jamil asked.

Jessie nodded.

"Well, I reviewed the camera footage for the last week. At no point did I see any van or truck on the property with any name having anything to do with mold cleanup."

"So they're faking it," Karen concluded. "There is no mold problem."

Jessie shrugged.

"Never say never," she said, "but claiming that an entire section of the residential wing is too dangerous to enter because of hazardous mold spores is a good way to keep folks from going anywhere near there and inadvertently discovering a potential murderer."

Jamil frowned.

"What's wrong?" Jessie asked him.

He kept his eyes down as he spoke, as if he felt bad even voicing his thought.

"I don't want to be the wet blanket here. But aren't we kind of out on a limb with this? We've made a lot of suppositions, based on not that many facts. If we're wrong, it could go really badly for all of us."

Jessie thought about the twenty-two-complaint lawsuit she'd been served yesterday. Jamil had no idea how right he was. If they were wrong, Otis, and possibly Gilliard, would sue them until they were ground to dust.

She decided to keep that to herself. If they were wrong, and maybe even if they weren't, she was facing years in court. But Karen and Jamil wouldn't have to. She'd take the heat for all of it. There was no reason for them to pay the price for her wild speculation.

"You're right Jamil," she said. "So I guess we should find out if we're wrong. What time is it?"

"Eleven forty-seven," he said, looking at his watch. "Why?"

"Because Karen and I need to head out. We've got a search warrant to execute."

CHAPTER THIRTY ONE

Jasper waited until no one was around.

When he was sure the hallway was clear, he pulled down the zipper on the plastic tarp that sealed off the first floor residential wing from the rest of West House. It would look awfully suspicious if anyone saw him entering an area marked "off limits zone: hazardous material warning."

He opened the large doors that closed off the wing from the rest of the house and then walked down the hall to the bedroom at the far end of West House. Jasper had put Paul there because, other than his own personal wing, it was the most isolated part of the residence. It also had its own bathroom, dining room, and small entertainment room, making it perfectly self-contained.

He was carrying a bag with a lunch made up of a turkey, compote, and brie sandwich, hummus and carrots, a ripe peach, and sparking water. Ever since Sunday morning, he'd asked the kitchen staff to make him two of every meal, one of which he personally delivered to Paul.

He wanted to keep the circle of information small. No one else knew Paul was here, although Nancy clearly suspected something was up. She was the one who suggested the mold cleanup idea when he'd told her the residence needed to be cordoned off for several days. She pointedly hadn't asked any questions.

He knocked on the door and waited. Sometimes Paul made him wait a while before answering. Jasper found it increasingly irritating that he was a kind of servant in his own home. Luckily, this time Paul answered quickly and ushered him in. He was dressed in blue jeans, sneakers, and an untucked button-down dress shirt.

The guy didn't look great. Normally the actor was the picture of virility. At forty, his close-cropped brown hair was just starting to show flecks of gray. In the last three days, the flecks seemed to have multiplied exponentially. His usually ruddy skin was pallid. His brown eyes were bleary and had dark shadows under them. He still cut a strapping figure but it was undermined by his hunched shoulders and defensive slouch.

"I've got lunch," Jasper said, trying to buoy his friend.

157

"Thanks," Paul said. "But I'm not that hungry."

"You've got to eat something," Jasper insisted as he sat down in a chair in the dining room before addressing the real reason he was here. "And we have to get you out of here."

"Don't you think I know that?" Paul snapped. "I wanted to leave that night but all those frickin' people made it impossible to get out without being seen. I'm supposed to be on set in New Mexico tomorrow morning. If I'm not there, the questions start and I don't have answers."

Jasper nodded supportively.

"Good, then we're on the same page. Let me call for a car. We'll find a way to sneak you out and get you to the airport."

"Fine," Paul said. "We'll do it tonight when it's dark."

"I don't think we should wait that long," Jasper said. "Like I told you, we've got a stay in place preventing the police from searching the estate. But LAPD is fighting it. If they get it overturned, I guarantee they'll raid the place within minutes."

Paul seemed to consider the idea.

"What about all the cameras? If I leave in the day, won't they be able to look at the footage later and see me sneaking out?"

Jasper shook his head. He'd already told Paul this, but apparently with everything on his mind, he'd forgotten.

"No. Remember? The cameras in this wing aren't operational. Neither are the ones in the hedge maze out back. That's why I brought the gardener uniform by yesterday. You can put that on and you can leave through the West House back door. It's a straight shot to the maze. I'll give you a key and you can exit via the back gate. I'll have a car meet you there. It can take you to your house to get your clothes and you can go on to the airport. There will be no physical evidence that you were ever here. You can say you spent the whole time that you were in L.A. in your house."

Jasper could tell from Paul's expression that this was the first time he'd really registered the idea fully. He seemed to like it.

"Okay," he said. "That sounds good. I just need a little time to decompress before we do it."

"That's fine," Jasper said. "And if you need a little chemical assistance to decompress, I have something upstairs that I can grab—drinks or something heavier."

"That's okay," Paul said. "Because of all the training for the movie, I haven't touched a thing in six months. I have shirtless scenes. Got to look respectable, right?"

"Right," Jasper said, though his brain had suddenly fixated on something other than the kind of shape Paul was in.

He flashed back to their phone conversation the night Milly Estrada had died. Paul had said he'd taken something to amp up the moment and that he'd gotten too excited as a result. That was how he inadvertently broke her neck.

But if he hadn't taken any kind of drug in six months, then he'd been lying about being high on Saturday night. And if he wasn't high, that meant he'd killed her while he was completely sober. That suggested that it wasn't an accident at all, that he'd done it intentionally.

Jasper couldn't imagine why his friend would do such a thing, although he had mentioned something about Milly being his lawyer when he got in trouble once. Was this connected to that?

It occurred to him that he'd be better off figuring that out somewhere else, away from the man who had apparently intentionally killed someone with his bare hands. Jasper's own hands weren't entirely clean when it came to eliminating people who made his life difficult. But he'd never actually done it himself. Even the thought was appalling.

"I think I'll go check on getting a car set up for you," he said, standing up quickly.

When he looked over at Paul, he sensed that he had an issue. The actor was staring at him. His eyes were no longer bleary. In fact, they were shockingly alert. His whole body had gone from slumped to stiff. It was then that he knew Jasper had caught his mistake.

"You know what, buddy?" Paul said, using the buttery lilt so many movie fans had come to love. "Why don't you just make the call from here? No point risking someone overhearing you, right?"

Jasper felt something rare for him these days: fear. He tried to keep it in check as he responded.

"You know, now that I think about it, I'm not sure I have the number. I better check with Nancy."

Paul stood up. With both men at their full height, he had three inches on Jasper, not to mention a good twenty-five pounds.

"Just give her a call now. I'll wait."

He looked down at Jasper with the confidence of a man who always got his way. Jasper normally carried himself with a similar confidence, but something about the other man's size and desperation unsettled him.

"Sure," he said, flipping through his phone. "Oh look, I do have it after all."

"That's great, Jasper," Paul said. His voice was ice cold.

Jasper made the call, asking for the car to wait at the back gate. Then he turned back to Paul.

"Let me point out the route. Like I said, from the back door here to the hedge maze, and the gate beyond it, is a straight shot, three hundred yards north."

"I think you should take me, Jasper. I'll wear the gardener uniform to keep a low profile but you know the way. I don't want to get lost in that maze. And you know how the back gate opens better than I do. You've got the key. It just makes sense to have you lead me there."

Jasper felt the panic rising in his throat and gulped it down hard.

"But if they check the video later, they'll see me escorting a gardener around. It will look suspicious. We don't want to give them anything to work with."

Paul reached behind him and pulled something out of the back pocket of his jeans. It was a serrated steak knife, one that was kept in the dining room for easy access. Paul's smile disappeared.

"I think you should take me."

Jasper held up his arms as if in surrender.

"Hey, buddy, calm down. There's no need for anything like that."

Without warning, Paul swiped at one of his raised arms, slicing across his left forearm. Jasper gasped. Looking down, he saw that blood had already started dripping down his arm to the carpet below.

He started to scream in pain but before anything came out, Paul had him pinned against the wall, his free hand clamped over his mouth, muffling the sound. Jasper struggled to get free but the other man was much bigger and stronger. For the first time in forever, Jasper Otis was afraid.

"Better tie that off," Paul said. "Like I said, I think you should take me."

CHAPTER THIRTY TWO

Jessie was antsy.

It was 12:26. She and Karen were parked half a block down from the main gate of the Otis Estate, just out of view of the cameras. Behind them were two additional unmarked cars. Another block away, on a less-traveled side street, were four squad cars and a large truck that could knock the front gate over if required.

The search warrant was supposed to be approved in just over a half hour, which left her far too long to obsess. She decided to check in with Hannah to see how she was doing and sent off a quick text asking about her day so far. The answer came back fast.

Boring. Even on a day with sex traffickers and undercover cops, I still had to take a European History quiz. Lame. Going to lunch now. Good luck catching the bad guys.

Jessie said thanks and didn't mention how glad she was that Hannah's day was boring. It was vastly preferable to the alternative.

"How's she doing?" Karen asked, correctly guessing who Jessie was communicating with.

But before she could answer, her phone rang. It was Captain Decker. She answered immediately.

"Judge Rhone released his ruling overturning the stay early," he said. "It just came out. I'm forwarding it to you and Detective Bray now. Are you in place?"

"Yes, Captain," she said, doing her best to keep her voice professional, despite the excitement she felt bubbling over.

"Then get in there," he ordered.

Jessie hung up without replying. Her whole body vibrated with righteous determination. Finally, she had the go-ahead to take this bastard down.

Karen had already hit the gas. Jessie sent her pre-set text telling all the other units to execute the warrant, then strapped on her seatbelt and tried to remember to breathe.

*

Hannah was starving.

After she finished texting Jessie, she hurried to lunch. She was halfway to the cafeteria when Elodie caught her by the arm.

"What's up?"

"Change of plans," Elodie said. "Rico wants to meet you now. He's on the side street, waiting."

"Why?" Hannah asked, keeping her tone level even as she felt an unfamiliar pang of what she assumed was dread. "I thought we were meeting at the same corner as yesterday after school. Isn't he worried about the cameras seeing him?"

"He wants to shake things up," Elodie said. "And to be honest, he wasn't totally convinced by your sob story about your grandpa. He thinks you may be chickening out. This is your chance to prove you're serious. But you have to go right now. If you don't, he says to forget about it."

"Can I at least go to the bathroom first?" she pleaded.

"Can she?" Elodie asked, lifting up the phone she'd been holding at her side this whole time to reveal that Rico was on the screen and had been listening in.

"No," he said firmly. "You're in the car in two minutes or you're out."

He hung up. Elodie looked over at her.

"Please don't screw me on this," she begged. "If you work out, I get a nice commission. If you bail, I have to pay a penalty and it's not cheap."

Hannah knew she didn't have time to waver. Even looking like she had doubts might make Elodie warn Rico off. She had no idea if one or both of the undercover cops had eyes on her amid the swarm of kids rushing to get lunch.

In the end, she knew she had no choice. Unless she got in the car with Rico, there was no chance he'd lead her to his boss and no chance of stopping the trafficking ring that had Jessie so upset. Her sister was counting on her, so she moved.

She waited until she was out of Elodie's sight before texting the undercover cops at the numbers she'd been given. Marie, the female cop, had instructed her not to text her or Brian, the male cop, unless it was an emergency.

She typed an innocuous message, one that Rico wouldn't find odd if he insisted on looking at her phone, as quickly as she could and sent it just to Marie. It read: *Can't meet for lunch. Going off campus to see a friend. Later.*

Only seconds later, she got a call. It was Marie.

"Don't," the woman said emphatically. "It's not safe. This could be a trap."

"I don't have a choice," Hannah hissed back. "If I don't go, we miss our chance. I'll do my part. You do yours. Follow us. Bust them when we get there."

"I'm pulling you out," Marie said. "We'll just arrest Rico and go from there."

Hannah was about to round the last corner to get to the side street where he was waiting. If he saw her on the phone, she feared she'd spook him.

"No," she said forcefully, nearly shouting. "You do that and girls will die. We have a chance to stop that. I'll be fine. Follow me. Call for backup. Do whatever you have to do. But don't ruin this. And stay way back. He's already paranoid. You can be the hero or goat, Marie. If you don't let this play out, you'll get the blame. I'll make sure of it."

She hung up without waiting for Marie's reply, put her phone on silent, and stuffed it in her pocket. As she rounded the corner to meet Rico, she made sure she had the right expression on her face: anxious but not scared.

It helped that it was exactly how she felt.

CHAPTER THIRTY THREE

"We are not permitted to allow entrance without a valid warrant," the security guard said over the speaker beside the gate.

They'd only been waiting at the gate for twenty seconds but each one was precious, an opportunity for Jasper Otis to hide Paul Gilliard or sneak him off the estate. Jessie was about to respond but Karen beat her to it.

"We have a valid warrant, which we'll show you at the front door of the house. You can open the gate right now or we'll have the truck behind us knock it down. It's your call. You have five seconds to hit that button."

It only took two for the buzz to sound and the gate to creak open. Karen blasted through so quickly her car scraped the edges of the gate as it passed. They tore down the long driveway and dashed out, where they were met at the South House main entrance by Nancy Salter, who stood in doorway like a bouncer at a bar.

"You're trespassing," she yelled as they ran toward her. "If you don't want to be personally sued, I suggest you turn around right now."

"Too late for that," Jessie muttered to herself.

"We have a warrant," Karen announced. "You can move out of the way or be arrested right now."

Salter looked briefly startled before recovering.

"Show it to me, please," she said.

"You can come with us while we search. Or you can hang here with one of the officers, who can show you a copy. But we're coming in now."

Jessie stepped up so that she was face to face with Salter. The other woman was still taller than her, but she didn't seem all that intimidating anymore.

"Move now," Jessie said. "Or I will move you."

After a moment's hesitation, Salter stepped aside. Jessie darted past her and turned straight toward West House. She glanced back and saw that Karen was right behind her. To her surprise, Detective Purcell was there too, though he looked reluctant to participate. It took less than a minute to reach the plastic sheeting outside the residential wing.

"I'll open it," Jessie said to Karen. "Cover me."

"That area isn't safe to enter," Salter said, catching up to them.

Jessie looked back at her incredulously.

"Don't waste our time with that," she said. "You're on the hook for this too, Nancy. Show us which room he's in or you'll be charged as an accessory."

Salter shook her head.

"You already know that Jasper's residence is upstairs," she maintained.

"Not Jasper," Karen said. "Paul Gilliard—where would Jasper have put him?"

The genuinely surprised expression on Salter's face made Jessie reevaluate just how much she knew about what was going on. Involuntarily, Salter glanced at the end of the hall. Jessie ran in that direction. When she got to the last door on the left, she pressed her ear to it in the hopes of hearing voices. But there were none. Karen arrived seconds later.

"Check if it's locked," the detective said.

It was. She looked at Salter, who was just arriving, huffing heavily.

"Unlock it," she ordered.

The woman did so reluctantly. Jessie pushed the door open and Karen stepped inside with her gun drawn. Jessie followed her, as did Purcell and two uniformed officers. They searched all the rooms of the residence but found no one. Karen looked over at Jessie with doubt in her eyes. Jessie could tell she was worried they'd screwed up.

"Check the other guest rooms in the wing," Karen instructed the uniformed officers.

They hurried out.

"When did Otis tell you to have this area sealed off?" Jessie demanded of Salter.

"Sunday morning," Salter replied.

Jessie stared at her hard.

"I'm going to give you a chance here, Nancy. I'm guessing you didn't know Gilliard was the one in here. But you knew something was up. Did Jasper suggest the mold story?"

Salter looked at Detective Purcell for help but he was stone-faced. It appeared that he'd finally come around and was putting the job ahead of the power. Without anyone to support her, Salter seemed torn. But apparently the two women standing in front of her with weapons drawn were more impactful than her loyalty to Jasper Otis.

165

"He said he needed to make sure no one entered the residential area for a few days. I came up with the mold remediation suggestion. We had it done last year and still had the plastic sheeting in storage. I didn't ask what it was about."

"You realize your boss has been hiding a murderer?" Karen said. "And that he may be helping him to escape right now? You need to tell us everything you know."

"I don't know anything else," Salter insisted. "Jasper has been very closed-mouthed the last few days. I had my suspicions but nothing firm, so I didn't ask."

As Karen continued to press her, Jessie walked around the residence, looking for anything she might have missed earlier. By the front door in the dining area, she saw a fresh stain on the floor, reinforcing her belief that someone had been here recently. Maybe they'd spilled some food. She knelt down and the unexpected smell of blood hit her nostrils.

Glancing around, she saw a small trail of droplets leading into the entertainment room and then the bedroom. Then they stopped, as if someone had found a way to staunch the bleeding. On a hunch, she walked into the bathroom. It seemed unremarkable. She walked over to the hamper and opened it. Inside she found pants and a shirt. The latter was covered in blood, as if it had been used as a tourniquet.

"In here," she yelled.

When Karen and Salter arrived, she pointed out the clothes.

"Whose are these?" she asked.

Salter's eyes widened.

"That's what Jasper was wearing," she said, clearly concerned.

Jessie's worry that she'd misjudged the nature of the situation only increased.

"It looks like your boss may have gotten on the wrong side of the man he was trying to protect. If you want to help him, your best bet would be to tell us where he might have taken Gilliard. His life might depend on it."

Salter thought for a moment, then shook her head.

"I honestly don't know," she said. "I assume they would have left via the private door over there to avoid being seen by staff. But after that, I don't know."

Jessie hurried over to the door, which she'd originally missed, as it was cleverly disguised as a wall panel. She opened it and looked outside to discover that it had a clear view of nearly the entire back of the estate. From here she could see the edge of the pool, the petting zoo, the hedge maze, and even a few guest houses. They could have gone anywhere.

She tried to picture Gilliard looking out from this same spot. Where would a desperate man, holding another one hostage, go? How could he best avoid detection?

"Is there a back way out of the estate?" she asked Salter.

"Yes," the woman said. "There's an alley that runs along the back of the entire estate and a connecting gate just beyond the hedge maze."

It was like fireworks suddenly went off in Jessie's head.

"Didn't you say that the only parts of the estate where the cameras are never on are the private residence and the hedge maze?"

"Yes," Salter confirmed. "Jasper often used it for...liaisons and didn't want them recorded."

Jessie turned to Karen.

"Let's go," she said.

CHAPTER THIRTY FOUR

Hannah knew something was wrong.

Rico seemed fidgety. There was none of the chilly confidence of yesterday. In fact, it seemed to Hannah that he was scared.

"Are we going to be back by one thirty?" she asked. "I have a calculus test fourth period."

That wasn't true but she wanted to keep the guy talking, anything to get a clue as to what he was thinking.

"I wouldn't count on it," he said. "These interviews take a while. You'll probably have to make it up."

"But it will be an unexcused absence," she protested, as if she didn't have any idea that something far more significant was happening.

"Look," he said, clearly agitated. "Karl wants to talk to you. If you want this setup to work, stop worrying about some test. This is bigger than that."

"So if Karl likes me, I'm in?" Hannah asked, trying anything she could think of to get Rico to give up more details. She suspected that if he wasn't so agitated, he would never have mentioned Karl's name.

"Maybe," he said. "But I think you're going to have a hard time doing that."

"Why?" she asked.

He looked over at her, clearly debating how much to share. Even before he spoke, she knew the answer. He'd passed along her name to Karl or whoever was in charge. Maybe Rico didn't know what they'd learned about her but they'd obviously told him to bring her to them ASAP.

Maybe they wanted to determine if she was just a rebellious teenager acting out by doing something illicit. But more likely they wanted to learn if her famous profiler sister knew about any of this. She doubted they'd ask her nicely. And based on the way he was behaving, Rico knew he was delivering her to people who had ill intent.

"You just don't seem totally into this," he finally said as he turned off the Pacific Coast Highway and started up a winding road

168

overlooking the Pacific Ocean. "I think they want to look you in the eye and see if you're really serious."

They were nearing the top of the hill, where the road dead-ended at a massive gated mansion. Hannah wanted to look in the side view mirror to see if the undercover vehicles were behind her. But she knew that would draw Rico's suspicion. Besides, if they were any good, she wouldn't see a thing.

"Is this it?" she asked as the car started to slow.

He nodded. Hannah realized that once they entered the property, she'd be stuck. The gate walls were easily ten feet high. Even if the cops were right behind her, by the time they got in, Rico's bosses would have enough time to do her all kinds of harm.

This was her only chance to bail. The car would have to stop while the gate opened. She looked over at Rico, whose hands were clenching the steering wheel so tightly that his knuckles were white. He was terrified. This was bad. She undid her seatbelt before reaching over and grabbing the passenger door handle. Nothing happened. It was locked.

"What the hell?" Rico said, looking over at her with confused anger.

If he pulled out a gun, she was trapped. She felt as close to scared as she had since Jessie's ex-husband tried to kill her. It was a rare and almost welcome emotion.

"I'm so nervous," she said, trying to salvage the situation. "I think I'm gonna throw up. You've got to let me out for a second."

"We're here," he protested. "Just wait a minute until we get inside."

"If you make me wait, there's gonna be puke all over your car," she told him, lifting her hand to her closed mouth as if she was trying to hold it in.

"Jeez, okay. Hold on!"

He popped the lock. She opened the door and got out, facing back down the hill and doubling over. For a second she thought she might actually vomit. Her whole body pulsed with excitement. Her heart was beating fast. She had goose bumps. There was perspiration on her forehead. She was nauseated and exhilarated all at once. It was amazing.

After a moment she sensed she wasn't going to throw up after all. But she had to make it convincing so she made retching sounds as she looked back down the hill. A hundred yards away, she saw an unremarkable sedan idling. Behind her, she heard the sound of the mansion gates creaking open. Glancing over to make sure Rico couldn't see her, she waved frantically for the car to come.

That's all it took. The car peeled out, its tires squealing as it sped up the road. She saw that Brian, the undercover cop, was at the wheel. He sped past the passenger side of the BMW, only feet from where she was crouched, and came to a sudden stop next to the right gate door, making it impossible for it to close. He hopped out and pointed his gun at the driver's side of the car.

"Hands in the air," he shouted, before adding, "You by the passenger side door, lie on the ground."

She didn't know if he was saying that for her protection or to maintain the illusion that she wasn't a part of this. Either way, she complied.

"What's going on?" she heard Rico demand.

"Step out of the car," Brian ordered.

Seconds later, four more cars came tearing up the hill. Two were unmarked. The other two were squad cars. As they approached, the sirens started blaring. One unmarked car and the two squad vehicles shot up the driveway without slowing down. The other unmarked car came to a stop right behind the BMW. Marie stepped out with her weapon drawn.

Hannah couldn't see what was happening but could clearly hear more orders, including "lie down," "spread your hands," and "don't move." Three more squad cars, all with sirens echoing through the canyon, zipped by. Eventually Marie came over and knelt down next to her.

"Are you really going to be sick?" she asked.

"No," Hannah said.

"Then you can get up," Marie said. "I'd like to get you out of the road so you're not accidentally run over."

Hannah sat up and looked around, taking in the scene.

"Are we sure this is the place?" she asked. "Did we get them?"

Marie took a moment to take in everything as well.

"Let's hope so," she said. "Otherwise we just ruined a perfectly good pool party."

*

As Hannah stood on the sidewalk near the gate, one ambulance tore out of the estate, followed quickly by another, and a third after that.

Though she couldn't see inside, Hannah was sure they were transporting the enslaved girls to the hospital.

After that, the squad cars drove out with men in the back. Up near the house, she could see others being led to cars in handcuffs. She didn't recognize them but waved anyway.

"Don't do that," Marie hissed. "You don't want to make yourself a target."

"What do you mean?"

"If we don't convict all of them, some might come looking for payback. We need to get them all to fall, like a series of dominoes, starting with your friend Rico."

The words had barely left Marie's mouth when Hannah got an idea. She knew exactly how she could ensure that Rico would turn on his boss and get those dominoes falling.

These were horrible men and they had to pay, even if it required her to cut a few moral corners. Just the thought of it made her giddy, almost like she was high. She knew in that moment that she would never stop chasing this feeling.

CHAPTER THIRTY FIVE

Jessie got to the maze first.

Somewhere behind her, she could hear Karen on her cell phone, instructing some officers to meet them there and others to go to the back alley. She tried to block all that out and focus on what was in front of her. The green walls of the maze were about seven feet high, too tall for her to see over as she rushed in.

As she made her way through, she scanned the ground, looking for blood drops even as she hoped to hear either man's voice. But the foliage seemed to suck up all the sound so that the only things she could hear were her own footsteps and shallow breathing. Karen's voice wasn't even audible anymore.

The maze was too dark to see any blood but she did notice something else. A narrow strip of grass was visibly pressed down more than the rest, as if it was more highly trafficked. The obvious conclusion was that this was the route most often used by someone who knew the maze well.

She bent down, doing her best to follow the same path while still keeping an eye on what might be around each bend. Each twist and turn took her closer to the center of the maze. As she curled around an impressively zigzagging stretch of wall, she heard Karen's voice call out from somewhere nearby.

"Jessie, where are you?"

She was just debating whether or not to respond when the zigzagging ended and she found herself in the middle of the maze, where an ornate fountain periodically shot a spray of water out of a stone dolphin's blowhole, making a loud whooshing sound.

Lying on the ground next to the fountain was Jasper Otis. He was on his back and looked to be unconscious. She moved carefully toward him and knelt down. There was a large pool of blood by his left forearm but his chest was rising and falling. He was still alive.

As the blowhole shot another spray of water into the air, she sensed movement nearby more than heard it. Spinning around, she saw a metal blade slashing toward her head, and flung herself backward. The knife missed her but the force of her movement sent her careening back and she felt her head slam into the side of the fountain.

Dazed, she looked around, attempting to get her bearings. Gilliard, wearing a gardener's uniform, was advancing toward her. She raised her right hand to fire before realizing that she'd lost her gun. He was almost on her when Karen called out again, this time from much closer.

"Jessie?"

Gilliard spun around and looked in the direction of the voice. He moved toward it quickly.

"Knife," Jessie screamed as she tried to scramble to her feet. "He's got a knife."

Gilliard crouched at the edge of the hedge as Karen came into view. She was looking the wrong way.

Time seemed to stand still. Jessie flashed back to the moment only months ago when she watched helplessly as her ex-husband plunged a knife into the chest of her partner, the man she loved. Now it was all happening again. Another partner was about to be attacked and she was too far away, powerless to stop it.

But almost as quickly as she had the thought, she rejected it. It wasn't true. She wasn't powerless. This didn't have to end the same way. She could stop it. She had to try. All at once, the world sped up again.

"Behind you!" Jessie shouted as Gilliard lunged at Karen.

Her partner turned around and managed to get her arm up in time to block the knife as it came toward her. But the blade embedded in her arm and the gun dropped from her hand. Karen let out a bloodcurdling scream.

Jessie tried to ignore it as she ran toward Gilliard, who was attempting to yank the knife out so he could stab Karen again. He'd just ripped it from her flesh when Jessie dove at him from behind, slamming her shoulder into the small of his back. As he lurched forward into the hedge, his body bent back in an unnatural "U" shape. Now it was his turn to scream.

His arm, knife included, was tangled in the branches of the hedge. He seemed unable to extricate himself. Jessie got to her feet and punched him in the kidney. He groaned and dropped to his knees. As he did, his face slid down, scraping along the hedge. But he was still holding the knife.

"Drop it," she yelled.

He wouldn't let go. Suddenly all the pent-up fury that had built up over the last few days spilled out of her. She would not allow someone else to be hurt on her watch. She would stop this, no matter what.

She didn't have a weapon on her so she proceeded to punch the arm holding the knife, first the triceps, then the elbow. When he still wouldn't release the knife, she began pummeling the same spot at the elbow junction over and over again. She lost count after a dozen blows. Finally he loosened his grip and the knife fell to the ground, too deep in the hedge to be reached.

"Step back, Jessie."

She looked to her right. Karen was sitting on the ground with her knees up. Her right arm was propped on her right knee, aiming her gun at Gilliard. She used her left arm to steady her right.

Jessie did as she was instructed. She was breathing heavily and her right arm felt like it was about to fall off. But Karen looked worse off. Her eyes were opening and closing slowly as if she might pass out.

"Mind if I hold that for you?" Jessie asked.

Karen glanced over at her, her eyes cloudy.

"That's probably a good idea," she said.

Jessie stepped toward her, taking the gun with one hand as she eased Karen back with the other. Her right forearm had a massive gash in it. Jessie thought she saw bone. She wanted to attend to the wound but couldn't do anything until Gilliard was secure. So she did all she could for now. Pointing Karen's gun at Oscar-winning actor Paul Gilliard, she yelled as loud as she could.

"Here! We're in here!"

*

Jessie almost enjoyed the ambulance ride.

This was the rare time that she'd been in one where she wasn't the one being attended to. Though her head hurt and she was told she'd need a CT scan at the hospital, the EMT was pretty sure she didn't have a concussion. So she was able to sit beside Karen and offer moral support.

The detective had been stabilized. She had an IV in one arm. The other arm, where she'd been stabbed, was heavily bandaged. She'd need surgery at the hospital. But for now she was doped up on pain meds and smiling woozily.

174

Somewhere behind them, Jasper Otis and Paul Gilliard were in their own ambulances. Otis had lost a lot of blood and was still unconscious, but he would survive. Gilliard would eventually recover too, maybe in time for his trial. But it wouldn't be easy.

They'd later learn that his diagnosed injuries included a fractured vertebrae in his lower back, facial lacerations, and, most surprisingly to the doctors, a broken arm. Apparently Jessie had punched him so hard and so often in the same place that the bone had cracked.

Jessie was just allowing herself to close her eyes for a moment when her phone rang. She looked at the screen but didn't recognize the number. Deciding this wasn't the time to be cautious, she answered it.

"Jessie Hunt," she said.

"Ms. Hunt, this is Officer Marie Gattis. I was assigned your sister, Hannah."

"Is she okay?" Jessie demanded immediately.

"She's fine," Gattis assured her quickly. "But we did have a little excitement."

"What does that mean?" Jessie asked, trying not to lose her cool.

"She's with me now. I'll let her fill you in on the details. But the gist is that multiple arrests have been made, including Richard 'Rico' Carter. We're en route to the station so Hannah can provide a statement."

"Regarding what?"

When the response came it wasn't from Gattis.

"Jessie, we did it!" Hannah shouted through the phone.

"Please," Jessie begged. "Someone tell me what is going on before I completely lose it."

"Don't be mad at me but I went with Rico. It's a long story but he took me to the house you talked about, the one by the ocean. Marie and the other officers raided the place. They arrested a bunch of guys. There were girls being kept there, like nine or ten. We stopped them, Jessie!"

Listening to the excitement in Hannah's voice, Jessie decided to go with it. She could press her or Officer Gattis for the details later. Right now wasn't about that.

"That's fantastic," Jessie said. "And you're sure that you're okay?"

"Yeah. It was a little scary there for a while. Rico tried to rape me. But the cops came before he could."

"He tried to what?"

"I'm okay, Jessie. Really, I wasn't hurt."

"All right," Jessie replied, willing herself to remain calm. "I'm glad you're okay. I have to take a colleague to the hospital but I'll meet you at the station a little later. Just stay close to Captain Decker, understand?"

When she hung up, Jessie saw that Karen was looking at her with a goofy grin.

"What?"

"You were a good parent there," Karen said, her voice cloudy. "You cared about how she was, not what she did."

"Karen, I'm not her parent. I'm her sister."

"I promise you. That's not what she thinks."

CHAPTER THIRTY SIX

Beto Estrada sounded scared.

It was Wednesday, a day after the raid on the Otis Estate. Jessie was in the Central Police Station conference room, waiting for everyone else to arrive, when she got the call. It came through over the conference room phone via the station front desk.

"Are you all right?" she asked.

"I'm not sure," Estrada said. "Is everything I saw on the news last night true? Did you really break up that trafficking ring?"

"Part of it," she said. "We haven't rolled everyone up yet. I'm actually a little surprised to hear from you. Should you be calling me?"

"I'm using the cell phone of a colleague at the firm," he said.

"So you're still worried?"

"Shouldn't I be?" he asked. "I didn't see anything about our mogul friend being arrested."

"It hasn't happened yet," she admitted. "We've got lots of people in the chain of command rolling over on their higher-ups. But no one's turned on him yet. In fact, right now he's got a lot of sympathy because of Gilliard's attack on him."

"Maybe I can help change that," Estrada said.

"What do you mean?"

"Like I said, I watched the news," he said. "For days, that man hid the guy who murdered Milly. He knew what Gilliard did. He needs to pay, and not just as some accessory after the fact."

Jessie, despite what he was saying, refused to allow herself to get too excited.

"What did you have in mind—would you like me to drop off Milly's personal effects?" she asked, referencing the coded phrase she'd suggested he use if he wanted help.

There was a long silence in which Jessie knew the man was deciding whether he was really ready to pull the trigger on a choice that would change his life forever.

"I think we can dispense with the euphemisms, Ms. Hunt. Do you still have that friend in the FBI, the one who could help protect me?"

"Of course," Jessie said.

"Could he protect someone else too?"

"Who would that be?" she asked, keeping her voice level.

"The source who gave me that audio file."

"I think that could be arranged," Jessie promised. "Shall I have your source picked up?"

"No need. She's here with me now. We're currently in a secure office at the firm. Ajax and three of his closest friends are with us."

"That seems wise," Jessie said, finally allowing herself to get keyed up. "Did you say 'she'?"

"Yes," Estrada replied. "I think it's safe to tell you now. My source is Maura Shore, the widow of Detective Brian Shore. We met a few months ago at a charity function to help find housing for young girls who'd been snuck across the border to serve as sexual slaves. When she learned that I was an attorney, she entrusted me with the file. She had no idea my firm represented some of Otis's business interests. I never told anyone about the file, not even Milly."

"So Milly getting killed at Otis's home was unrelated to this?" Jessie asked.

"I believe so," Estrada said. "I don't think he even knew about the file until I passed it along to you. He may have been surveilling you because you questioned him about Milly's death. It was just an unhappy coincidence that we discussed the file while he was having you followed."

"I apologize again for that," Jessie said.

"You couldn't have known," he said. "It's hard to fully comprehend the reach of a man like Otis until you're in his crosshairs."

"But you do and Mrs. Shore does too and you're still willing to come forward?"

"It's time for this to end, Ms. Hunt," he said. "I haven't gotten a good night's sleep since I heard Marla's voice. Between me and Maura Shore, that should be enough to tie Otis to these cases and to her husband's murder."

Jessie nodded, though no one could see her.

"Sit tight," she said. "I'm going to reach out to the bureau now. Expect a call from Agent Jack Dolan soon. He'll work out the logistics of bringing you in. And Mr. Estrada?"

"Yes?"

"Thank you."

By the time Captain Decker and Gaylene Parker walked in ten minutes later, everything had been arranged. Jessie decided not to fill them in just yet.

"How's Detective Bray doing?" Decker asked as he took a seat at the conference table.

"They think she may have escaped nerve damage," Jessie said. "The knife blade got a little muscle but mostly bone. She'll be on desk duty for a while after she returns but she should be back in the field in a couple of months."

"I'm glad to hear that," Decker said. "And you were cleared—no concussion?"

"Just a bump," Jessie assured him. "It's actually my hand that feels worse. It's so bruised that I can't even make a fist."

"Please don't," Parker said, feigning alarm. "I don't want to get knocked out by Sugar Ray Hunt."

Before Jessie could crack back, Jamil walked in.

"Sorry for being late," he said. "I just had to wrap something up."

"Such a slacker," Jessie joked.

"Don't give him a hard time, Hunt," Decker said. "He just verified who the mole is."

"Wait," Jessie interrupted. "Is it safe for us to be discussing this here?"

"We had the whole station swept this morning," the captain replied. "They found multiple listening devices throughout the station, including in here. But we should be good now."

"Okay, then don't keep me in suspense," Jessie said. "Who did all this?"

"Fred Timmons," Decker announced.

Jessie searched her memory, but came up empty.

"I have no idea who that is," she said.

"He's a deputy desk sergeant," Parker said. "He usually works nights and the weekend shift."

"That's how he was able to do all this surreptitiously," Jamil added. "The station was usually at about one-quarter capacity when he was on duty and he had easy access to lockers, surveillance footage, logbooks, and schedules."

"And he just did it for the money?" Jessie asked.

"According to his bank account, it looks like he's been getting payments for the last two years," Jamil said.

"He was originally paid to bury those cold cases we uncovered," Parker said. "He couldn't destroy them but he misfiled some and hid others. So when Otis's people found out about the Marla audio file, they already had someone in place to steal it."

"Is he willing to turn on Otis?" Jessie asked.

"I doubt he ever interacted with the guy," Decker said. "But Trembley's working on him in interrogation now. If he turns on his boss, maybe we can work our way up the line."

"That seems to be the order of the day," Parker said.

"How's that?" Jessie asked.

Parker smiled broadly for the first time since the meeting started.

"It's partly because of your sister. Everybody we caught at that house yesterday is climbing over each other to make a deal. That Rico fella tried to hold out for a while. He kept saying your sister made up the sexual assault claim against him. But when he found out that she was the kid sister of the legendary Jessie Hunt, he changed his tune. He knew we'd go to the mat on that. Truthfully, I think he would have kept his mouth shut if not for her."

Something about that stirred an uncomfortable feeling in Jessie that she couldn't quite place. The idea that Hannah had made the exact allegation against Rico that was most likely to get him to cave, an allegation that was based on her word alone, seemed awfully convenient. There was no way she was going to question her sister about her claim that a man had tried to rape her. But something about it just felt...wrong.

"People are coming clean left and right, it seems," she said, aggressively moving on.

"Who else?" Decker asked.

Jessie told them about her call with Beto Estrada. It got Gaylene Parker especially excited.

"Having Detective Shore's wife come forward could be extremely powerful," she said, "especially since we may be able to corroborate the suspicion that he was killed. I've been having our vehicle expert review all the data on Shore's car. It's not definitive yet, but he thinks it's possible that an explosive may have been used to sever Shore's brake line when he was driving up the mountain."

"That would be huge," Jamil said.

"Yes," Decker agreed solemnly. "He deserves justice, even if it was delayed for years. Parker is looking into who at West L.A. Division might have been involved."

Parker nodded. The smile was gone.

"What's wrong?" Jessie asked her.

Parker looked at Decker, who nodded for her to go ahead.

"I don't want to ruin our celebratory mood, but it looks like not everyone is going to get justice," she said.

"What are you saying?" Jessie asked.

"I was interviewing Elodie Peters and I mentioned the name Marla. She recognized it. She gave us the girl's real name, hoping it would get her some leniency."

"Who is she?" Jessie asked, using the present tense though she feared that was too optimistic.

"Her real name is Marlene Janice Cooper. Elodie said that they were recruited around the same time. They went on several overseas trips together. On one of them, when they were both seventeen and losing their cachet because they were too old, Elodie said Marlene was pumped with heroin. It was done purposefully so that a client could have his way with her while she overdosed. He wanted to reach sexual gratification while she was in her death throes."

Jessie closed her eyes, hoping to somehow push the image Parker was describing out of her head. It didn't work. When she opened them again, she saw that both Decker and Jamil were looking away. But Gaylene Parker was staring at her, head up and eyes clear, full of righteous anger. This was why she was a Vice cop—to stop this kind of thing.

"What happened?" Jessie finally asked.

"She died with the john on top of her," Parker said. "Afterward, they weighed her down and dumped her in the river. Elodie named the john too."

"Who?" Jessie asked. "Was it Otis?"

"No. But he was there. It was Sultan Omar Abdul Salah."

Jessie sat with that for a moment before responding.

"Can anything be done?" she asked.

"Elodie seems willing to testify against Otis," Parker said. "She told me that she was terrified they'd do the same thing to her they did to Marlene, so she made herself invaluable, even after turning eighteen. She claims to have recruited more girls in the last two years than most of the other high school recruiters combined."

"What about Salah?" Jessie asked.

Parker shook her head.

"We've already put in a request for his extradition to the State Department," she said. "But they're not optimistic. They say that as long as he doesn't return to the U.S. or visit a country that has an extradition treaty with us, he's probably untouchable."

Jessie exhaled deeply, nodded, and stood up.

"If that's all for now, I think I'm going to take the rest of the day off," she said.

Decker walked her to the door.

"Once you've had some time to decompress, I'd like to discuss how we can get you back soon. Remember, I'm shorthanded."

"Captain," she said, trying to sound diplomatic despite feeling exhausted to her bones, "I have a seminar to teach on Friday. I'm supposed to start a new one next week. My boyfriend is learning to walk and talk again. My sister was just used as bait in a sex-trafficking sting. You might have picked the wrong moment to broach this."

"There's never a right moment, Hunt."

"Maybe not," she conceded. "But I'm not going to think about any of that right now. We'll talk later. I have some people at home I need to hug."

CHAPTER THIRTY SEVEN

Ryan made dinner that night.

Admittedly it was just grilled cheese sandwiches, but Nurse Patty said it was part of his physical therapy and he seemed quite proud of the accomplishment. Kat, deciding that both Jessie and Hannah needed a bit of a break, came over to assist.

When they finally sat down to eat, it felt almost like a holiday. In addition to Jessie, Ryan, Hannah, and Kat, Jessie asked Patty to stick around for dinner even though it was officially Nurse John's shift. Jessie snuck her an extra fifty bucks for her trouble. They even had to bring in a couple of folding chairs from the garage to accommodate all six of them.

Everyone was in a good mood.

"I think we know who the real chef in this house is," Ryan teased Hannah.

"Don't get cocky," Kat shot back at him on her behalf. "Until you can make something that's not a middle school cafeteria staple, she's still got the belt."

"Is this some kind of fancy cheese?" Hannah asked, feigning wide-eyed innocence at Ryan's culinary accomplishment.

"Yes," he answered. "It called 'melted.'"

The two nurses, sitting next to each other, compared notes quietly and Jessie swore she heard Patty utter the phrase "amazing improvement."

She didn't talk much herself, preferring to just bask in the glow of the closest thing she'd had to a real family experience in forever. She even pretended not to notice that nearly being sexually assaulted seemed to have had no discernible impact on Hannah, who was giddy after her role in bringing down a sex trafficking ring.

By the time Kat and Patty left, the rest of them, save for John, were wiped out. Hannah said goodnight and headed to her room. As John got Ryan ready for bed, Jessie did one last check on her sister.

"I don't want to pressure you," she said, sitting down on the edge of the bed, "but do you want to talk about what happened?"

Hannah shook her head.

183

"Not really," she said. "Maybe down the line, but right now I just want to focus on the positive, you know?"

Sure," Jessie said. "I totally get that. Still, I'm going to make an appointment for you with Dr. Lemmon for tomorrow after school. Be as forthcoming as you want or say nothing at all. Either way, I think you should at least have a chance to unload whatever's on your mind."

Hannah nodded noncommittally.

"See you in the morning," she said, effectively ending the conversation.

Jessie sensed that something was off but she couldn't quite put her finger on it. Part of her wondered if she'd just spent so much time worrying about her sister that it had made her paranoid. She was tempted to push a little more, but ultimately chose not to. There'd be time for that.

"Goodnight," she said, ordering herself to get up and walk out without another potentially alienating word.

She left Hannah's room and returned to Ryan's, where John was just finishing up. The nurse stepped out, leaving them alone for the first time all night. They sat side by side on the edge of the hospital bed, not talking for a while, just holding hands.

"Have surprise for you," Ryan finally said.

Jessie marveled at how much clearer he sounded in just the few days he'd been home.

"What is it?" she asked.

"Stand there," he said, pointing to a small "X" taped on the ground about five feet away from the bed.

She got up and moved over to the spot.

"Face me," he instructed.

She turned around.

"Watch this," he said.

Then, with great effort, he grabbed the walker beside him and pushed himself up off the bed. Jessie, fighting the urge to rush over to him, kept her legs locked in place. He wavered slightly as he looked down at his feet, then looked up and winked at her.

Without a word, he took a small, shuffling step with his right foot, then another with the left. He clutched the walker so tight that his knuckles turned white. After about twenty tiny steps and nearly a minute, he was standing directly in front of her.

"Want to dance?" he croaked.

She laughed, allowing herself a rare, full-throated moment of pure joy.

"Yes," she said. "I absolutely do."

He moved the walker to the side and put his hands on her shoulders. For a moment she thought he might actually try to dip her.

"Next time," he said, his eyes bright but his breath slightly labored. "Taking rest of the week...off. Too pooped."

It was the first time they'd been standing together face to face in forever and she couldn't let the opportunity slip by. Wrapping her arms around his waist, she leaned in and kissed him. Then, very slowly and carefully, she guided him back to bed and tucked him in. He was asleep before she left the room.

Jessie returned to the guest room, which she was increasingly hopeful was only a temporary arrangement. She got ready for bed, climbed under the sheets, and turned out the lights. And then, within moments, she too was asleep.

And unlike so many recent nights, she didn't have a single nightmare.

EPILOGUE

He waited until the young man had settled in for the evening before he started.

By the time he rang Jared Hartung's doorbell, he'd already spent several hours in the man's house, preparing for the events to come. But none of that planning diminished the excitement of this moment.

It had been years since he'd engaged in a true hunt. For the last two decades, he'd been reduced to the occasional use of the homeless to sate himself, but no longer. After seeing Jessie Hunt, the protégé of his long-time nemesis, Garland Moses, on the news, he'd been inspired. He was ready to resume his work.

"Yes?" Jared said when he opened the door, barefoot and wearing a UCLA T-shirt and sweatpants.

"I'm so sorry to trouble you, young man," he replied, playing up his hunched back and raspy voice. "My car conked out on the street just over there and my cell phone seems to have died as well. I was hoping I might borrow your phone to call the auto club."

Jared seemed torn between civic duty and the desire not to be bothered when he was trying to relax.

"Um—" he started.

"I promise not to be a nuisance. After I call for assistance, I'll wait in the car. I don't want to disrupt your evening."

That reassurance seemed to persuade Jared.

"Sure," Jared said. "The phone's in the kitchen."

He stepped inside, and Jared closed and locked the door.

The old man smiled. That was one less thing for him to take care of later. He followed Jared into the kitchen, delicately removing the syringe from his jacket pocket when the younger man looked the other way. In the other hand, he held his wallet at the ready.

"There you go," Jared said, pointing at the phone.

"Thank you so much," the old man said as his wallet dropped from his hand onto the floor between them. "Oh dear, I'll get that."

He started to bend over, moving as slowly as he could. Jared only let a moment go by before he caved.

"Don't worry. I've got it," he said, bending over.

186

The second he did, the old man plunged the syringe into Jared's exposed neck and took a step back. Jared popped back up immediately, a confused, angry look on his face.

"What the hell?" he demanded.

"I saw it," the old man said with concern. "I think it was a wasp. Did it sting you?"

"A wasp?" Jared repeated, already looking slightly unsteady.

"Yes," the old man assured him. "Are you all right? Maybe you should sit down for a minute."

He pulled out a breakfast room chair for Jared, who nodded and took an uncertain step in that direction. The old man knew that if Jared fell to the floor, he'd have a devil of a time getting him back up, so he offered a hand, which Jared took. Once the young man took another step toward the table, everything clicked into place.

The old man used Jared's own momentum and pulled hard on his arm. Jared banged into the table and collapsed onto it face first. As he moaned, the old man lifted his legs up on the table and, with much effort, rolled him onto his back.

Then, as Jared watched with terrified eyes, he moved over to the cabinet and removed the toolbox he'd left there earlier that afternoon. He placed it on the table beside Jared, who couldn't move a muscle but could see clearly.

The old man opened his box and removed an X-Acto knife, which he used to carefully slice open Jared's T-shirt. He studied the young man's chest. It was hairier than he preferred but that could be rectified.

"Whahhhoo?" Jared managed to groan, an impressive feat considering that he shouldn't have been able to make any sound at all at this point.

"So many questions," the old man said sympathetically. "I promise, very soon you'll have all the answers."

He put down the knife so that he could slide his gloves on. Then he selected his preferred tool and looked back at Jared.

"It's time to begin," he said.

And with that, the Night Hunter got to work.

NOW AVAILABLE!

THE PERFECT FACADE
(A Jessie Hunt Psychological Suspense Thriller—Book Twelve)

"A masterpiece of thriller and mystery. Blake Pierce did a magnificent job developing characters with a psychological side so well described that we feel inside their minds, follow their fears and cheer for their success. Full of twists, this book will keep you awake until the turn of the last page."
--Books and Movie Reviews, Roberto Mattos (re *Once Gone*)

THE PERFECT FACADE is book #12 in a new psychological suspense series by bestselling author Blake Pierce, which begins with *The Perfect Wife*, a #1 bestseller (and free download) with over 500 five-star reviews.

A group of suburban moms go out to a high-end hotel in the big city to celebrate their 40th birthday, and the night gets wild—too wild. When they wake from their sordid night to find a dead body amongst them, Jessie must unravel what happened that night. Could the murderer be one of them?

Or are they being targeted?

A fast-paced psychological suspense thriller with unforgettable characters and heart-pounding suspense, THE JESSIE HUNT series is a riveting new series that will leave you turning pages late into the night.

Books #13 (THE PERFECT IMPRESSION), #14 (THE PERFECT DECEIT) and #15 (THE PERFECT MISTRESS) are now also available.

Blake Pierce

Blake Pierce is the USA Today bestselling author of the RILEY PAGE mystery series, which includes seventeen books. Blake Pierce is also the author of the MACKENZIE WHITE mystery series, comprising fourteen books; of the AVERY BLACK mystery series, comprising six books; of the KERI LOCKE mystery series, comprising five books; of the MAKING OF RILEY PAIGE mystery series, comprising six books; of the KATE WISE mystery series, comprising seven books; of the CHLOE FINE psychological suspense mystery, comprising six books; of the JESSE HUNT psychological suspense thriller series, comprising fourteen books (and counting); of the AU PAIR psychological suspense thriller series, comprising three books; of the ZOE PRIME mystery series, comprising four books (and counting); of the new ADELE SHARP mystery series, comprising six books (and counting); of the EUROPEAN VOYAGE cozy mystery series, comprising six books (and counting); of the LAURA FROST FBI suspense thriller, comprising three books (and counting); and of the ELLA DARK FBI suspense thriller, comprising three books (and counting).

An avid reader and lifelong fan of the mystery and thriller genres, Blake loves to hear from you, so please feel free to visit www.blakepierceauthor.com to learn more and stay in touch.

BOOKS BY BLAKE PIERCE

ELLA DARK FBI SUSPENSE THRILLER
GIRL, ALONE (Book #1)
GIRL, TAKEN (Book #2)
GIRL, HUNTED (Book #3)

LAURA FROST FBI SUSPENSE THRILLER
ALREADY GONE (Book #1)
ALREADY SEEN (Book #2)
ALREADY TRAPPED (Book #3)

EUROPEAN VOYAGE COZY MYSTERY SERIES
MURDER (AND BAKLAVA) (Book #1)
DEATH (AND APPLE STRUDEL) (Book #2)
CRIME (AND LAGER) (Book #3)
MISFORTUNE (AND GOUDA) (Book #4)
CALAMITY (AND A DANISH) (Book #5)
MAYHEM (AND HERRING) (Book #6)

ADELE SHARP MYSTERY SERIES
LEFT TO DIE (Book #1)
LEFT TO RUN (Book #2)
LEFT TO HIDE (Book #3)
LEFT TO KILL (Book #4)
LEFT TO MURDER (Book #5)
LEFT TO ENVY (Book #6)
LEFT TO LAPSE (Book #7)

THE AU PAIR SERIES
ALMOST GONE (Book#1)
ALMOST LOST (Book #2)
ALMOST DEAD (Book #3)

ZOE PRIME MYSTERY SERIES
FACE OF DEATH (Book#1)
FACE OF MURDER (Book #2)
FACE OF FEAR (Book #3)
FACE OF MADNESS (Book #4)
FACE OF FURY (Book #5)

FACE OF DARKNESS (Book #6)

A JESSIE HUNT PSYCHOLOGICAL SUSPENSE SERIES
THE PERFECT WIFE (Book #1)
THE PERFECT BLOCK (Book #2)
THE PERFECT HOUSE (Book #3)
THE PERFECT SMILE (Book #4)
THE PERFECT LIE (Book #5)
THE PERFECT LOOK (Book #6)
THE PERFECT AFFAIR (Book #7)
THE PERFECT ALIBI (Book #8)
THE PERFECT NEIGHBOR (Book #9)
THE PERFECT DISGUISE (Book #10)
THE PERFECT SECRET (Book #11)
THE PERFECT FAÇADE (Book #12)
THE PERFECT IMPRESSION (Book #13)
THE PERFECT DECEIT (Book #14)
THE PERFECT MISTRESS (Book #15)

CHLOE FINE PSYCHOLOGICAL SUSPENSE SERIES
NEXT DOOR (Book #1)
A NEIGHBOR'S LIE (Book #2)
CUL DE SAC (Book #3)
SILENT NEIGHBOR (Book #4)
HOMECOMING (Book #5)
TINTED WINDOWS (Book #6)

KATE WISE MYSTERY SERIES
IF SHE KNEW (Book #1)
IF SHE SAW (Book #2)
IF SHE RAN (Book #3)
IF SHE HID (Book #4)
IF SHE FLED (Book #5)
IF SHE FEARED (Book #6)
IF SHE HEARD (Book #7)

THE MAKING OF RILEY PAIGE SERIES
WATCHING (Book #1)
WAITING (Book #2)
LURING (Book #3)

TAKING (Book #4)
STALKING (Book #5)
KILLING (Book #6)

RILEY PAIGE MYSTERY SERIES
ONCE GONE (Book #1)
ONCE TAKEN (Book #2)
ONCE CRAVED (Book #3)
ONCE LURED (Book #4)
ONCE HUNTED (Book #5)
ONCE PINED (Book #6)
ONCE FORSAKEN (Book #7)
ONCE COLD (Book #8)
ONCE STALKED (Book #9)
ONCE LOST (Book #10)
ONCE BURIED (Book #11)
ONCE BOUND (Book #12)
ONCE TRAPPED (Book #13)
ONCE DORMANT (Book #14)
ONCE SHUNNED (Book #15)
ONCE MISSED (Book #16)
ONCE CHOSEN (Book #17)

MACKENZIE WHITE MYSTERY SERIES
BEFORE HE KILLS (Book #1)
BEFORE HE SEES (Book #2)
BEFORE HE COVETS (Book #3)
BEFORE HE TAKES (Book #4)
BEFORE HE NEEDS (Book #5)
BEFORE HE FEELS (Book #6)
BEFORE HE SINS (Book #7)
BEFORE HE HUNTS (Book #8)
BEFORE HE PREYS (Book #9)
BEFORE HE LONGS (Book #10)
BEFORE HE LAPSES (Book #11)
BEFORE HE ENVIES (Book #12)
BEFORE HE STALKS (Book #13)
BEFORE HE HARMS (Book #14)

AVERY BLACK MYSTERY SERIES

CAUSE TO KILL (Book #1)
CAUSE TO RUN (Book #2)
CAUSE TO HIDE (Book #3)
CAUSE TO FEAR (Book #4)
CAUSE TO SAVE (Book #5)
CAUSE TO DREAD (Book #6)

KERI LOCKE MYSTERY SERIES
A TRACE OF DEATH (Book #1)
A TRACE OF MUDER (Book #2)
A TRACE OF VICE (Book #3)
A TRACE OF CRIME (Book #4)
A TRACE OF HOPE (Book #5)

CPSIA information can be obtained
at www.ICGtesting.com
Printed in the USA
LVHW111156160821
695402LV00001B/59